AFTER THE FIRE

AFTER THE FIRE

A novel

DANIEL ROBINSON

THE LYONS PRESS
Guilford, Connecticut
An imprint of The Globe Pequot Press

The Lyons Press is an imprint of the Globe Pequot Press.

Printed in the United States of America

10 9 8 7 6 5 4 3 2 1

ISBN 1-58574-760-2

The Library of Congress Cataloging-in-Publication data is available on file.

To all of the men and women who fight wildfires

"after the fire, a still small voice"

—*1 Kings 19:12*

Of the many people whom I would like to thank:

My crew supervisors—George Marcott, Lonnie Williams, Leonard Wehking, and Jon Larson—whose guidance kept us out of trouble and who all taught me a great deal about leadership.

Kyle Torke and Josh McKinney, who read the very first draft of this novel and told me that it was good enough to keep at it.

John Pratt, Rikki Ducornet, and Bill Wiser, who taught me more than I can ever acknowledge.

Lilly Golden, who proves that there still are great editors.

Sandra Lea and Caitlyn.

Chapter One

MONDAY

That night's visitation had pulled all the sleep from Barnes. He woke well before sunrise and remained awake. He listened to the rainwater slap against the concrete sidewalk and felt the roughness of his unshaven face with his hand. He once loved spring—regeneration and renewal in everything from nature to baseball to love. He used to feel that way a lot, almost swollen with the anticipation of spring. Then he would wake early to greet the morning, his coffee cup full while he stood on the back deck as the sun tossed early streamers of light through the branches of trees and the day opened to the heat that would eventually arrive. That morning, though, while listening to the remnants of the last rain or the predictions of the next, he felt no sensation for spring, no anticipation, no want.

Barnes allowed the telephone to ring. It stopped after the fourth ring and an empty moment later the answering machine recorded Ruth's voice. "Barnes? Are you there? Are you going to work today?" A moment later she added less solemnly, singing even, "Get out of bed you sleepyhead, and shake a leg or two. The sun is up, pour some coffee in the cup."

The machine hummed in silence before clicking off.

Barnes smiled and rolled from bed. He rubbed his feet on the morning coolness of the wood floor. He pushed the play button on his answering machine as he walked past and let it repeat Ruth's message.

Showered and shaved and dressed in clean Levi's and a T-shirt, Barnes retrieved the newspaper from his front porch. The morning air carried a sachet of smells—lilacs and wet dirt and the scent of a fire from a distant fireplace.

Light falling through the waved glass of the dining room's windows drew altered images across the room and table. In a line, shoulders and arms touching, the twelve who died sat silently on the heating radiators beneath those old windows—Chandler first, for he was the foreman at the bottom of the line when they were burned over, then Dago, Sully, Budd, Hassler, Earl, Freeze, Lopez (who should not have even been with Chandler's squad), Horndyke, Stress, Doobie, and Warner.

"Again this morning?" Barnes asked to the ghosts.

They stared at him in silence.

A few hundred times, Barnes thought, a few hundred times you go to a fire. The weather is always hot and dry, the winds are predictable mostly in that they will change, the fuels are dried, the slopes are steep. Two hundred fires like that and nothing happens, maybe a flare-up, maybe you beat a hasty retreat to a safety zone. But, still, two hundred fires. And then.

And then every little thing conspires.

What happened? What did you do? What did you not do? The questions held tight in each dead crewmember's blackened eyes as they stared at him. Where were you? Barnes heard them ask.

Bracing himself against the table, Barnes looked at the dozen ghosts silhouetted by the back light from the windows. He shook his head. He knew he had nothing to say that could matter, nothing that he had not already tried to say, so he turned and flicked on the light switch. Before they faded off in the room's new light, however, his ghosts stood and walked from the room. They walked close enough to Barnes that he could have reached out and touched them had they possessed form.

Chandler again led the way. The others followed out of the haze of light cast from the sun shining through a window. They walked without noise, no words spoken, their heavy boots touching silently on the wood floor. Each held Barnes's eyes for a moment before letting the next capture him. Behind the last of Barnes's crew were Max Downey and Russell Fleming, the two jumpers who had also died.

Barnes studied each face as it passed from the dining room into the soft darkness of the front room. Their faces were clear, more clear in his memory than in his sight, but clear just the same as they looked at him. Lopez, dark hair, dark skin, dark eyes, offered him the same shy smile she gave him every morning of the two fire seasons they had known each other. Stress looked down on Barnes and nodded his head, and Doobie had the chemically distanced look that Barnes knew was not there that afternoon the previous summer but which Barnes had seen plenty of nights when they met each other off-duty at a downtown bar.

The early sun cast a veiled light into the hallway. Barnes followed them. He listened to the groans and cries of his wood floors, shifting calls like a great weight had been placed then lifted from the floor. He walked with the slowness of age, an old man anticipating an end around the corner.

The weight and the lightness of death stood before him. The finish. Answers to questions. Dark holes. Deepness. End.

Barnes drove that Monday afternoon. He had no place to drive, no particular reason to be driving, but he drove anyway. He drove a circle of streets that bordered the older parts of Fort Collins.

The buildings he passed told him a story of his town. Along Laporte they mixed in eclectic and personal style, a syncopation of designs from old stone houses still strong and sturdy on their sandstone foundations to newer houses, mostly small ranch styles holding college renters. Some of the houses handsome with ivy having grown for sixty years over their brick or stone or stucco and trees planted by a child on her birthday grown to shade the entire yard, some of them folding in upon themselves from too much use and not enough care like an old person giving up hope or a rose nearing its end, some of them with names from their first families, and all with histories to tell for those who cared to listen.

Farther south, the houses became less individual, more like boxes a slowly passing train had kicked out in preset increments. A pair of railroad tracks snaked along the eastern boundary of his circle anticipating a freight laden with new cars going north or old scrap heading south. Not far from where the railroad tracks split was where the first Fort Collins had stood, a picket-fenced outpost the cavalry had established in the alamo of cottonwoods and willows along the banks of the Poudre River. A park had been built near that small long-gone establishment and its parking lot was where Barnes had lost his virginity in the camper shell of his first pickup truck.

Claire, her name was. Claire with hair the color of cornsilk, a woman still in her teens with much to teach a young man eager to learn. She liked to talk, but that was not what she liked to do most. He drove near the parking lot and thought about Claire and how he would have told her about the fire and wondered whether she would have cared before or after she opened her legs for him.

She seemed remote, not just and simply because she was nearly two decades into his past nor because she had long ago married some ski bum in Vail and written a last letter telling him to not write again, but because everything seemed remote to him as he drove alone in the town. His world was far away from her and far away from the person he used to be.

"No big deal," Chandler had said above the heavy whop of the helicopter's main rotor. "We'll knock this dog's dick in the dirt."

The rotor whirled clockwise above them as they hovered above the fire. Max Downey, the smokejumper in charge of the fire, sat in the front of the helicopter, with Barnes and Chandler in the rear seat. The pilot had dipped the helicopter in a steady turn around the fire's perimeter so that the three could take a simultaneous look.

"Ain't no-thing," Max Downey had said.

"If you tie your line into that diamond-shaped area, you may have it," Barnes had offered.

"We got it dicked," Max had said absently.

Counterclockwise, opposite the helicopter's rotor or the helicopter's steady turn, Barnes drove the circle of streets in Fort Collins. He sat high in his 1950 Chevy pickup above the rest of the crowd for his twenty-five-minute circuits.

Crossing College Avenue, he accelerated to make it through the light. The day had turned hot and dry, a welcomed heat following the rains. He opened the hood vent to force more air into the truck's cab and leaned into the air coming in his opened window.

Two Hispanic men continued to work under the hood of their car on West Laporte Avenue. Each time Barnes drove past them they had switched places. First the tall guy with the ponytail had his head under the hood and next the short one in a muscle shirt was buried in the engine compartment.

On his third circle, Barnes saw a tow truck pulled up in front of the car, "Hooking for a Living" scripted in bold red letters across the back of the tow truck's cab. The two Hispanics were laughing and talking with Nick, the owner of Nick's Towing and a one-percent biker with MS. Barnes sounded his horn, and Nick turned unsteadily, placing a hand on the bed of his truck. Nick waved at Barnes. Barnes smiled and waved back, happy to again see that Nick did not allow the injustice of life's hand to keep him down.

Barnes turned on his radio as he passed the city's police station. Once, back when the police station was not there and he and Claire would spend hidden hours in parking lots, he had driven home from the old Dirty Sam's Nightclub while Claire, almost passing out, gave him a blow job. The combination of six inches of new snow, half again as many bottles of Coors, and her making love to him sent the old truck sliding drunkenly into the curb.

They might talk, he thought, if he could find Claire and bring her back along here where she helped cause him to bend the front axle on his first truck. Initially, they would not talk about the fire or any fire, just about her life in Vail or wherever she now lived. They'd laugh like conspirators as they remembered the road and the snow and the night and the curb. She might ask about the purple scar along the outside of his wrist and he'd just say it was one of those things, "part of the job," something safe like that.

With her next to him, her eyes closed and her leaning back to let the sun's warmth laze on her like a soft quilt, they would circle the city. He would slip a reference to some fire into the conversation.

"What's that?" she would ask or "Where was that?" or, better, "Tell me about it."

"Something that happened," he'd say as they turned from Laporte south onto Overland Trail, the foothills beginning their crawl on the truck's right and the gaping smile of Horsetooth Rock poking above the hills to the southwest.

"What?" Gently, with the touch of her hand on his thigh, she would lean to him. "Tell me."

Slowly he would begin to talk about fires. About the fire near Prescott, Arizona, where, after twenty hours of humping along and digging a line across a parched ridgetop, he stood lookout on a rock watching the fire grow. The fire which had that morning appeared tired and weary, a middle-aged fire readying itself for retirement, erupted to youthful life as it began a ravenous run up the ridge, devouring each new clump of fuel with a vigor and ever-increasing stretch of its grasp. About how he saw first the fire's smoke column roil in intensity and darken from gray to charcoal and about how he then called to warn his crew boss, for he was then a squad boss on an Alaska crew. How his crew and two other crews working with them filed into a safety zone and watched the fire cross their line like nimble little Jack jumping the candlestick.

He would tell her about being treed by a protective black bear sow or chased by a cow moose on fires in the Yukon Flats. And about the national park fires that often turned into public-relations fires because an ignorant public knew less about wildfires than about quantum mechanics and wanted something done, something they could watch on the evening news. And about how they dug their firelines down to mineral soil, which could be hip-deep or deeper if the fire was on the Olympic Peninsula, or how the firelines in Alaska turned to mush and mud because there was no mineral soil, only permafrost to expose to the sun. And about the fire above Naches, Washington, where he stepped into a stump hole in the middle of the night and buried his calf nearly to the knee inside an oven of heated ash and sand.

"Sounds exciting," she would say. People always said that when he told them what he did for a living, all except that fat banker at the credit union who leaned back in his chair to study the loan application Barnes had filled out to buy the house next to Call's. The banker who rested the corpulent jowls of his triple chin on his chest and said, "When are you going to get a real job?" Barnes offered to show the banker a dose of reality across the street in the government parking lot. Both the loan and his offer were turned down.

When she would say, "Sounds exciting," he would smile. He would look at her and her hair the color of cornsilk blowing in the truck's wind and then past her at the fallow fields stretching the half-mile to the rocky beginnings of the foothills.

"Sometimes," he would say. "Sometimes it was exciting. Those were the best times, being close to death and feeling the hot winds of its breath on you and then being alive. But," he would add quickly, not yet ready to talk about what was obviously coming. "But mostly it was just long hours with your head in the dirt. Sometimes the most flame you'd see for days on end would be some cigarette smoker's match. Sometimes you'd be walking around all day long with the rain coming down in buckets and you're hunched inside your raincoat just hoping to find a hot spot to open up and stand in because your feet are too damn cold."

"Were you ever scared?" she would ask, pausing briefly as her voice slid into sadness and concern. "Were you ever scared for your life?"

And he would tell her about the time near Fairbanks when Leonard, his crew boss then, turned to Barnes and said, "I don't like this." Together they were leading the crew up a muddy fireline when the world turned silent and dark. Just as Barnes answered, "I don't like it either," the scrubby forest of black spruce turned into orange flags of flame. They ran, quite literally for their lives, through the mud of the fireline to a safety zone a hundred yards back.

"What a man," she would tease as she squeezed her fingers tight around his thigh.

Barnes would smile again, a smile colored with some embarrassment.

"What?" Claire would ask, serious now.

He would look at her.

"What?" she would repeat. "Why did you call me up?"

"It didn't always end good."

"What happened?"

A shrug weighted heavily with memory.

"Do you not want to talk about it?"

"I do, but let me catch my breath."

"Okay. Take your time. I'm not going anyplace."

Barnes had nothing to hurry him. So he drove leisurely through the falling afternoon. No hurry. The air blowing inside the truck's cab was cooling but the box heater had somehow turned on. Barnes made a note to fix that thing again before it burned him up in the heat of the approaching summer.

Barnes turned onto Prospect, heading east and away from the mountains. A half-dozen college students waited at a bus stop. They all wore shorts and ballcaps and colored T-shirts and carried day-packs over their shoulders. Their mouths moved but, as though they were in an old Japanese B-movie, no sound came from them. A couple of them laughed and one punched another on the shoulder. Barnes thought it must be about three-thirty and the kids were waiting for the bus to take them to their four-o'clock finals. Business majors or pre-vet students, something safe and sustained like that, Barnes thought. For a moment he envied them for that.

He thought he might ask, "You want me to tell you about Warner? He was the closest to the ridgeline, close enough that he probably could see the blue of the sky looking straight at him as the fire rolled over him. You want me to tell you about him?"

"If you want to," Claire would say. She would have turned to face Barnes, her hair loose and alive in the wind.

"He would have lived had he used his fire shelter. The official report says so, but I knew it as soon as I saw his body, bent over on hands and knees with his forehead touching the ground as if he were praying. Next to him, like it was ready for use, lay one of his plastic water bottles . . . with water still in it. It wasn't melted. It was good. His hardhat was only partially melted. Except for maybe a quick blast of heated air, the temperature couldn't have gone much above four hundred degrees. Under his shelter, he could have made it easy, like lying in a loud sauna."

"But you can't be responsible for him not having his shelter out."

He neared a girl on her bicycle. She wore bright biking shorts, a running bra and visored cap. Her movement was certain and steady. Barnes could see as he pulled up behind her that beads of sweat had formed around the elastic rim of her top. He whistled, but the wind caught his sound and dispersed it like color into the sky.

"If I would have checked him, though, I might have saved him," Barnes would say to Claire. He imagined squinting at her through the sun's blaze which would be, as the sun was then, staring through the truck's rear window over his shoulder.

"How? Checked him how?"

"I made everyone carry their shelters on their pack belt. Warner liked to put his shelter in the back of his pack and put an extra canteen and some munchies in the shelter pack on his belt. I'd caught him on the fires in Idaho doing that and made him give me twenty-five push-ups on the line in full gear. We joked about it, and I knew he'd switch them again if I didn't bite his ass about it. If I would have checked his shelter case while we were at the base heliport, I'd have caught him. And that would have saved him."

"But still . . . you can't be expected to think of everything."

"But I did think of that. I saw him stacking his gear and yelled to him, asked him where his shelter was. He said, smiling, 'For Christ-sake, Barnes, I already got a mother—it's where it's supposed to be.'"

"So he lied."

"I knew, though. I knew. Two minutes of my time, a walk of twenty-five feet—that's all. I just didn't want to hassle with it, is all. I was just too tired to save him, and, goddamnit, I even thought that. I thought, 'Go ahead and burn up, you stupid bastard.' I thought that."

The sun had lowered as he turned left again from Prospect onto Lemay. The high blast of a siren startled Barnes and he realized that he could not remember driving the entire length of Prospect Road. He slowed his truck to the side of the road and watched as the ambulance passed him on its way to the hospital, nervous lights stabbing at him as it passed. He sped up again and drove on through the siren's receding wake.

"The noise never stopped," he would say to Claire. "When I was in the fire shelter waiting for the fire to pass us by, it never stopped. And I couldn't stop it or the sounds I couldn't hear except as they yelled in my head."

Claire would not say anything then. She would have nothing to say, no way to talk with him, no words that would be more than words. She might look at him or she might look straight forward through her side of the truck's split front windshield.

Then he would tell her about another fire, a fire on which nobody died—the fire in Alaska when Leonard, his crew boss, was treed by a yearling black bear. Leonard had taken a couple of men with him to retrieve some cases of rations from a cache dropped by helicopter. Only problem was that this black bear had found the cache first.

"Usually," Barnes would say, "a black bear will run if you make enough noise, except this particular black bear either didn't understand the rules or just didn't care. Anyway, she had the poor taste to actually want to eat this stuff and was willing to fight for it. I saw Leonard and the others stand on a rise and start jumping up and down and waving their arms. Then, like someone had hit a pause button, they stopped all that, and for a second they were stuck in time. They ran into a clump of paper birch and over the rise came this black bear into the birch stand. Well, one of the guys, a big guy, climbed about the smallest birch tree and he was up there swinging back and forth like he was on the tip of a metronome. The bear chased him from side to side and just as he hit the end of his arc and started back up, the bear nearly reached him. He swung like that a couple of times before he caught another tree and climbed into it. The bear paced between the three trees holding these three guys, stopping under each tree to gaze up at its inhabitant. I let them hang for a few minutes before I gathered up my sawyers and we made enough noise to scare off the bear."

He imagined that Claire would have liked that story. It was a safe story, a happy ending story that let you feel good. It would have been a good story for Claire. Not the typical story of a fire; most fires were too nondescript for Barnes to remember. His fire record listed more than two hundred fires but he could only remember a third of those for something other than dirt and ash. Then there were the dozen fires when he had seen the possibility of death, and another half-dozen on which men had died, and the one that had killed half his crew. That story was not a story Claire would like. But she would listen.

He might have told Claire that he had paused, unable to say anything while his finger keyed his radio's mike. That for a few seconds he had watched the fire begin its run up beneath his crew and all he could say was, "God."

He remembered the terror in his voice sounding far away. He had heard and seen the fire ramp and tear at and above the land, the heat and smoke bite at the short scrub oaks and huddling bunches of piñon and juniper, and the small forest of brush and trees crack as if under a great weight. Those seven seconds of mute dislocation probably would have saved Warner, the man nearest the ridgetop, and might have saved Doobie and Stress and Horndyke and Lopez and maybe even Freeze.

He knew, as he drove past the city's hospital, how seven seconds, the distance of a full breath as he drove, might have saved some lives. That would have been hard to tell, and she would not have wanted to hear that.

Barnes took the turn easily and smoothly from Lemay left onto Riverside. The turn arrow had switched green just as he approached and he coasted around the corner as his truck creaked and groaned from its shifting weight. To his right were the railroad tracks. A lone man walked with his head down and a full and dirty pack on his back. The man's studied gait matched evenly with the track's ties. The man moved his hands and bobbed his head as though he were talking. As Barnes passed him, the man suddenly stopped and rotated his hand above his head in continuing counterclockwise circles, then just as abruptly he quit circling his hand above his head and pointed across the road, across Barnes's path and up as if he were pointing at a defining tower.

Barnes slumped to look beneath the rim of the truck's metal visor but he saw nothing other than treetops and soft cumulus buildup. When Barnes looked back at the lone man, the man had returned to his singular walk, head bent and bobbing and hands nervously dancing in the air ahead of him.

He passed a white Ford Mustang in the right lane. The Mustang's driver, an aging hippie, flipped off Barnes as he passed. Barnes felt this should be his last revolution around the city.

He felt like having a drink. He really felt like having half a dozen drinks, but a couple bottles of cold beer on the porch as the sun rested behind the Front Range sounded good.

He slowed to let a pedestrian cross Mountain Avenue into the shops and bars of Old Town. Barnes thought of Claire and their winter evenings spooning in darkness after the wildness had passed, of how they talked about living in a cabin somewhere without roads, of having no one but each other. An old dream worth carrying.

He could have told Claire how he stood in the ash and stubble surrounding Warner's body. He knew Warner was dead when he saw the man lying, crouching almost, thirty yards from the ridgetop. As he approached Warner's body, he saw Warner's yellow aramid shirt had been burned from his arms and the skin discolored and charred. He watched the rigid body for movement but saw none. He thought of how still, how stiff the body remained as a light wind blew ash in tiny swirls. Warner looked like he was hiding his eyes with his hands, like a kid playing hide-and-seek, but his hunched body stayed so stiff. Charred shreds of the shirt and T-shirt rimmed the singed nylon belt at Warner's waist. His hardhat lay a dozen feet away from him, most of the painted red feather had been burned away but the quill pointed uphill with the hardhat's bill toward Warner. His green fire pants had been stripped from butt to boot top and the man's legs were stained with death.

Barnes had circled the body and found Warner's left glove still on his hand. Warner had already told Barnes that he would be leaving the crew at the season's end. "One last summer of fun," Warner had said one afternoon in Idaho as he and Barnes mopped up a stump hole together. Warner had graduated from Colorado State that June and would begin law school in Boulder that autumn.

He would tell Claire how, on that day in Idaho when they mopped up together, Warner had seen a squirrel stumbling over twigs and through the ash. They both watched for a few minutes before going to the animal and Warner picked up the squirrel. Its eyes had crusted over from tears mixed with ash. Warner carried it to the fireline, where Barnes opened his water bottle and poured some onto the squirrel's head. Warner rubbed the water into its face until the layer of ash screening its sight dissolved and washed away. Warner set down the squirrel in the green outside the line and it quickly scurried up the first spruce. Neither man had spoken during those fifteen minutes, and they remained silent as they walked back to the stump hole they were digging out.

That would have been a good story for Claire, Barnes thought. That would have been a story she could have hugged him for.

He turned the corner from Mountain onto Loomis and slowed to a halt against the curb. The afternoon had turned calm and lazy, a dignified idling he could feel on his closed eyelids as he sat in his truck's cab in front of his house. He opened his eyes a slit and could see inside the dust swirling in his front room the figure of Warner watching him.

He saw Ruth alone in the near corner of her porch, the same afternoon light transient around her. Barnes traced her shape against the backdrop of budding lilacs and red brick, watching even at the distance of tens of feet her breathing, or imagining her breathing.

Ruth's husband, Robert, walked past her like a stranger straggling through the week, neither looking at her nor turning to speak to her. And Barnes could see that she also did not acknowledge him.

Robert took the front steps two at a time. At his car, he turned and waved, a brief smile on his face, before he drove away. Ruth answered his wave with a tentative wave of her own. Then both hands returned to her cup. She watched Robert's car disappear around the corner. She took a sip from her cup.

Ruth did not watch Barnes as he walked to her house. She offered him no recognition as he neared her. She stood with her hands around her coffee cup, looking down toward the age cracks in the porch.

During his last revolution around town, he had stopped at Steele's for some groceries. He self-consciously swung the bag between his hands as he approached her.

"He's leaving me," Ruth said.

"Robert?"

"Yes. He's leaving me."

Ruth placed her cup on the porch ledge and brought her soiled hands together to rub them as though the day had suddenly turned cold. Barnes watched her eyes dart across a planter that had been recently turned and weeded, as though she were forcing part of her mind to concentrate on something other than Robert, searching out new dandelions or bindweed or snow-on-the-mountain creeping in to strangle out her columbines and cosmos.

Barnes did not know what to say. He watched the slight whiffs of steam rising from Ruth's coffee cup. He knew "I'm sorry" was wrong, and he knew "Are you all right?" sounded trite because she obviously was not. He thought he might tell her that everything would be okay, but he did not know what would be right, and he sensed that she knew a more certain truth. He stood watching her eyes move and said nothing.

Then Grace walked through the front door with a cup of lemonade in her hands. "Hi, Barnes. What'cha doing?"

Grace was five years old with, like her mother, brown almond-shaped eyes but blonde, not brown, hair tinted by a blush when the sun lighted in a soft angle across her head. She was active and precocious, and Barnes liked her more than he thought he would like a little kid.

Barnes smiled at Grace. He had once told her that, no matter what, he would always have a smile for her. He leaned down toward her and said, "I was out for a drive and saw your mother over here, so I thought I'd come over and see what kind of trouble you're getting into."

"No trouble." She held the lemonade in both hands as she drank.

"No trouble? Then what?"

"Helping."

"You do that well." He stood back up and smiled at Ruth.

"Right," Ruth said, extending the word in sarcasm. "As long as it's green and growing, she pulls it. She's not just weeding parts of the flower bed, she's denuding them."

"Clean cut," Grace said between drinks of lemonade.

"Clear cut?" Barnes asked.

"That."

Ruth said, "A little more selectivity is called for here, sweetheart." She shrugged her shoulders at Barnes in a sign of parental resignation, knowing that Grace probably would not register the difference between good green stuff and bad green stuff.

Barnes looked down at the sun bouncing from Grace's hair, a new blossom on the stem. Grace looked back up at him with a smile somewhere between happy and trouble.

Breaking the silence, Barnes asked Ruth, "Aren't you working at the library today?"

"I called in sick. Tomorrow too."

Barnes nodded. He understood that slough Ruth seemed to have fallen into. He wished that he could help her find her way out.

Ruth bent to her weeds and said, "Talk with you sometime tomorrow?"

"Yes. But now I had better get this home before my ice cream melts."

"Ice cream," Grace sang. "I scream, you scream, we all scream for ice cream."

"You come over this evening and I'll give you some."

"Okay, Barnes."

"We'll talk later," he said to Ruth, feeling something like a thief who had stolen a moment from her and left only an empty space in replacement.

Ruth let out a heavy sigh. Her eyes slid up from the ground to Grace and to Barnes. She gave him a somber smile. "I'll talk with you tomorrow," she said again in a tone that was closer to questioning.

"Yes," Barnes said.

Ruth took Grace's hand and led her back inside their house.

As he mounted the steps to his own house, Barnes heard the hard metallic sound of a car door being shut in anger. He turned and saw a man wearing cowboy boots and a Stetson walk toward him from across the street. Barnes had never met the man, but he knew immediately who he was. Even had he never seen the man's photograph repeated in newspapers and magazines and on television, Barnes would have known that this man was Max Downey's father.

"You Barnes?" Downey's voice was heavy and condescending.

"Yes." Barnes watched Downey's eyes tighten. Downey stood tall and straight, his shoulders squared like a man who felt he could best life through his presence. He left his hands at his sides, and Barnes could see the tension in Downey's jaw.

"I'm George Downey. We have to talk." The man's tone slid into demanding. He sounded like someone used to getting his way, a businessman who gave orders and offered no opportunity for excuses or questions.

"About the fire?" Barnes asked with some hesitation. He knew what about but he still asked, an attempt to draw off Downey for the moment in order to gather his own thoughts. Downey's son, Max, was the smokejumper in charge when the Red Feather Hot Shots helicoptered up to the helispots above the Tempest Ridge Fire. Max had made the decision to put in the fireline, digging a direct line down the hill with the fire burning below the crews. Max had made the decision but Barnes had agreed. Max had died on that fireline along with Russell Fleming, another jumper, and the twelve members of Barnes's crew while Barnes watched from a helispot further up the ridge.

"I'm going to court," said Downey.

"I heard." All of the newspapers along the Front Range as well as the Missoula newspaper had called for interviews. Barnes had ignored their queries and wished he could ignore Downey's.

"I want you to testify," Downey said. It was not a plea yet not quite a demand either, closer to an insistent suggestion.

Barnes brushed his hand through his hair. He said, "I don't know that I can help you, Mr. Downey."

Downey protested immediately as though prepared for some reluctance from Barnes. "By God, they want to crucify my boy. You knew him. He was as good a man as there is, and these sons of bitches have blamed him for what happened on that mountain. Blamed him, damnit, blamed him."

"I can't help you," Barnes answered again.

There was a dry pause through which Barnes could feel himself and Downey fall into opposing silences. Barnes had read the newspaper articles that blamed him for the deaths and the articles that placed blame on Downey and the articles that placed blame nowhere. Some of them were right. He saw no reason, though, to go to court over those that were wrong or those that were right and someone wished were wrong. All he could see coming from that action were more heartaches for the families of those who died. So he kept his mouth shut, talking only to the official investigating team. The only other person he talked to in depth about the fire was Call, Ruth's seventy-year-old father next door.

"You won't help," Downey said. There was no resignation in his voice, as though he had known what Barnes would say and had resolved to carry on in spite of Barnes. Maybe, Barnes thought as he stood with Downey in the day's increasing heat, Downey preferred it that way. Barnes became the villain, the man who had made the wrong choice.

"I can't help you," Barnes repeated. "I don't see any good purpose in going to court."

"I see. You *want* people to think that Max fucked up so they won't blame you."

"No, sir, I don't want that. I just—"

"I know what you want, but this isn't just about you."

"What you're doing is—"

"Don't tell me what the hell I'm doing. I know what I'm doing.

I'm saving my boy. I couldn't save him then but I sure as hell can save him now."

"This isn't going to help anything."

"You mean it won't help you."

A hard silence separated them. Neither man had moved from where he had begun.

Downey's jaw muscles twitched. Barnes could feel a tightening in his own fists and arms, but neither man stepped into the no man's land between them. Barnes knew that a violence would most certainly follow such a closing. He kept his body as open as he could and his eyes tight on Downey's to keep that violence from occurring.

Barnes felt a weight of absence. In the weight of absence, he also felt his ghosts walk along that fireline with the trust of the blind.

"You got nothing to say," Downey said. Barnes thought whether the man meant it as a question or an accusation.

"No," Barnes said.

"We'll talk again."

Barnes said nothing.

"You're a coward and a son of a bitch. I'd haul your worthless ass into court if I didn't think you'd lie like the rest of them. You and all them office bureaucrats who wrote that damn report, you're all alike. Save your jobs, save your hides. Not a one of you is worth half my boy . . . not half, goddamnit, and you all know it."

Tears welled in the old man's eyes, and his entire body shivered with rage before he turned and walked back across the street to his car.

After Downey had driven off, Barnes gathered the day's mail—credit card applications, a Victoria's Secret catalogue that Chandler had gotten him a subscription to, his bank statements, and his Fidelity IRA statement. He sat at the dining room table with a bottle of Fat Tire. He opened the mail, but did not consider it carefully. He no longer kept a monthly track of his retirement accounts and investments. As had a great many other things, that practice had ended the previous summer.

He was tired. Downey's visit had drained him, and the previous night's sleep had been short and unfinished. He had woken from his dream drenched in his own sweat to lie naked on his back and watch the moon's light push shadows across his ceiling.

In that night's dream he was not down with them. Nor did he stand on the ridgetop above them nor hover in an unattached distance. He stood in the dirt of the fireline no more than fifty feet from the first of them, half the distance between that man and the ridgetop. He watched as a rush of heated air pushed them forward into the ground and the closest of them, Warner, knelt as in prayer while the fire rushed over him, melting his face like wax.

He had woken then with that image of Warner looking up at him. For the next two hours until dawn, he had remained almost motionless, his hands crossed under the back of his head and his feet searching cool places on the bed's sheets. Mostly, though, he had stared at the ceiling as it moved through a spectrum of sober colors from black through the grays to flat white.

For almost another hour after, he had continued to lie in his bed and stare at the spidered cracks in the plaster of his ceiling, sifting through black-and-white stills in his memory.

The one he had stopped on was a mental picture from the season's first fire, nine weeks before the fire that killed half his crew. They had assembled along a fallen Douglas fir log—some of them sitting on the dirt and dried pine needles on the ground in front of the log, some of them sitting on the log, and some standing behind it. Some slept, some ate apples or candy bars, some talked in slow whispers, some stared in mute exhaustion at Barnes as he walked toward them.

The faces on the sixteen men and three women looked out from behind various shades of dirt, their eyes heavy and drawn, their yellow Nomex shirts and green pants stained from dirt and sweat. They looked like warriors, and they looked like beggars heavy with age.

The fire stayed in the background—a serpentine line of black ash on the ground, charred fingers of blackened bark reaching up the sides of the trees, an unnatural brown to the needles of some of the pines, a lone lodgepole naked and bare of foliage with its skeleton standing like a lance.

Hardhats and chainsaws and Dolmars and daypacks and orange five-gallon water canteens and work gloves lay spread along the ground and log. Tools were stacked in neat piles of pulaskis and shovels. There was no hint of moisture on the ground nor in the air. Everything—the trees, the bushes, the ground, the firefighters— was parched.

The night before had been warm and dry with an inversion keeping the fire's heat in, and the fire had spread through the night in slow crawls and occasional quick surges. The crew had kept along, digging their fireline with a steady sureness. The sawyers in front of the diggers had cut a twenty-foot-wide swatch through the trees and high brush. The diggers followed, cutting their fireline three feet wide and bare to mineral soil.

A few times in the night, the shovels hurried to the front to knock down some flame. But mostly the night passed with the simple routine of a fire at night. The crew tied in their line as the morning began to warm and then were relieved by a hot shot crew from Oregon which would begin to mop up the fire.

The men and women of Barnes's crew, the Red Feather Hot Shots, rested against the log and waited for Barnes to join them before returning to fire camp, hot food, a few hours' sleep in the antiseptic light and heat of the eastern Oregon sun, and then on the line again that evening.

That, however, was never the picture formed in his dream. That image of his crew, tired and dirty after twenty-three hours on the line, was what he wanted to remember. The dream, though, drew a dozen of his crewmembers in death, a fire burning over them as they ran for the lost safety of the ridgetop.

Chapter Two

TUESDAY

B arnes had slept the night through with only the memory of his fire dreams. Memories that formed dents in his dreams, that scarred his conscience. With his morning coffee and newspaper in front of him on the dining room table and a suggestion of morning sunshine filtering across the window, he remembered dreaming of death but also of life. But he could not remember the dreams, just a sense of them as if they had been mailed and returned to him marked "Return To Sender—No Longer At This Address."

He read in the *Coloradoan* newspaper about an early-season fire in Alaska near Fairbanks. Although the newspaper gave no specifics on the fire other than an estimation of size, an estimation of containment, and the hysterics of civilians who lived near the wilderness yet wanted none of the wild, Barnes could visualize a tundra and black spruce fire burning behind a large column of gray-black smoke spiced with orange fingers of flame. He could see the members of the two Alaska hot shot crews, Chena and the Midnight Suns, going direct on the fire's flanks, standing ankle-deep in the water of a tussock field and beating out the fire's flames with gunnysacks and spruce boughs. Matier would be out front of the Suns and Thiesen in front of Chena watching the fire and their crews, directing a PBY-2 on where to make the next retardant drop, and scouting the line for the safest attack.

Thiesen had mentioned to Barnes over the winter that he hoped to leave the line and move into a management position. Barnes had thought then, and thought again as he sipped his coffee, about transferring to Alaska and taking the Chena crew. He knew then, however, as he knew that morning in his dining room, that turning his back momentarily on the questions of chance and death and terrible mistakes did not mean that those questions had fallen away; it just meant that they grew darker and deeper until he again would be forced to confront them.

The doors onto the second floor deck of Ruth's house swung open. Through his window, Barnes saw Call take one quick step onto the deck. Barnes could not see all of Call but could see enough to know that he was naked except for a pith helmet and a Red Ryder pump-action BB gun. Call stood in the morning's opening rays of sunlight, surveying the elm trees near Loomis Street and the eaves under his house's roofline.

The sight of a naked seventy-year-old man with his gun in his hand had suddenly arrested the morning's motions. Barnes, holding his coffee cup in suspension between table and mouth, watched Call take aim and pot a pigeon that had roosted on his house. Barnes could see Call shake his finger at the dead bird and yell to Harp, his dog, as the bird tumbled into the lilac bushes lining the fence. Call laughed and moved his finger in the air to chalk up another one for himself.

Barnes left his coffee cup on the table and called Ruth. She answered on the third ring and he told her about Call.

"Naked?" she asked, mystified.

"Except for the pith helmet."

"Pith helmet? Naked and wearing a helmet and shooting at pigeons with a BB gun."

"Got one, too."

"Killed a pigeon?"

"You got the picture."

"I'm trying hard not to."

"It's all, and I mean all, right there in living color."

"Why does he do that? He wakes up and shoots pigeons because he thinks they're the reason he didn't sleep well that night."

"Maybe they are."

"Maybe."

"Whatever the reason, you had best get him inside before one of the less understanding neighbors calls the police."

"Oh, hell."

"You want me to come over?"

"No. I don't relish the idea of facing a naked old man, especially my naked old man, but I'll talk him in."

Minutes later, after Call had returned to the house and Ruth flashed a wave down at Barnes, Barnes reread the article on the Alaska fire. He liked reading about fires. The stories filled him with a sense of immediacy and expectation, something like what Chandler had once said as they helicoptered into a fire in the Bitterroots. The snow-feathered mountains had stood in angular defiance behind the fire which was large and mean enough to send two separate and distinct smoke columns roiling toward heaven. Chandler had leaned into Barnes to yell over the humming-thump of the 214's twin engines, "Kind of makes your nipples hard, eh Barnes?"

Barnes did not need to read about fires to remember the previous summer's fire season. He only needed to close his eyes and he could see each fire flash before him, from the tragedy fire that killed half of his crew to the minor fire that began the season, an Oregon fire nine weeks before half his crew had died in that consumptive flame. That first fire in the Deschutes Forest near Sisters, Oregon, had been a good first fire—uncontained but slow-moving, mostly lodgepole and fairly flat. A fire they could work all the way through from the line construction of initial attack to gridding the burn searching out the last smoke.

Twice during the first night of that fire, someone, one of the crew's rookies—Freeze, Budd, or Horndyke—asked how much farther to the line's tie-in. Aggie, the crew's lead pulaski because she knew how to keep the line straight and fast, answered the same both times, "One hundred yards." After the second time of this, a couple of the crew's veterans mocked their rookies, asking how much farther.

Aggie answered, "You writing a book?" She lifted her head to look forward toward where the sawyers had cut the general direction of the line, then returned her gaze to the ground in front of her feet. She kept her back as flat as possible to minimize the strain of bending over for a dozen hours with little rest. That was her fourth year on the crew, and she hoped that the next fire season, if Chandler or Hunter moved on, she would become one of Barnes's squad foremen.

"I'm writing one," answered George, who worked the first shovel to clear the line following the four lead pulaskis. "You want to hear what your chapter is called?"

"If I thought you could write, I'd ask," Aggie said.

Kapell said, "We all know hot shots can't write or read."

George added, "Brute strength and ignorance."

A couple of people laughed, someone stretched out the bray of a mule, but most of the twelve crewmembers who composed the digging line just continued to dig.

Barnes spent the night well ahead of the crew, scouting the line and the fire, watching the progress of both and coordinating the movements of his Red Feather Hot Shots. Hunter stayed closer to the crew, streaming ribbons from tree limbs or brush stalks to mark where the fireline's center would run. Every so often, Barnes would wait and talk with Hunter about the fire and the ridgeline, and Barnes would point the direction before walking back into the night. Then Hunter would set the line as straight as he could into the darkness, walking ahead of his markers twenty-five or thirty yards to be certain the line was good before tying his streamers back toward the line, then walking ahead again, often calling in specific orders to White, who held the radio for the sawyers, or Aggie, who as lead-P also carried a radio, or to Chandler, the other squad foreman, who was tail shovel at the line's end kicking everyone in the butt to keep them moving along.

First to arrive at Hunter's ribbon line were the sawyers moving in a short bumping line of their own, although stretched out over a longer distance than the diggers. Monterey, the head sawyer, led the way, then Sully, second saw, Ira, third, and Dago, fourth. They cut every tree and large bush ten to twelve feet on each side of Hunter's ribbons. They felled every tree away from the fire to keep from adding fuel to it and sometimes walked an additional ten feet toward the fire to limb a dog-haired tree.

Following closely behind and sometimes with the saws were Budd and White, the swampers. They each carried a tool, Budd a shovel and White a pulaski, in case of a sudden flare-up near the sawyers. Swampers, or saw pimps as Chandler called them, were also mules as each carried a Dolmar, plastic containers with one gallon of premix fuel in one side and a quart of bar oil in the other. In their packs, besides the thirty-five pounds of gear that anyone else on the crew carried, they each had a couple of saw wedges, saw files, and an extra chain in case one of the sawyers broke his. Sometimes, as they did on that night, they also each carried an extra gallon of water in plastic orange canteens in case a crewmember ran short. White usually worked with Monterey and Sully while Budd usually stayed with Ira and Dago, hauling their cut trees and brush away from the fireline, bringing the Dolmar when one needed to refuel, and sometimes spotting one of the sawyers for a few minutes on the chainsaw to give the sawyer a quick break for a meal.

The swampers carried five pounds more than most of the diggers but five pounds less than Barnes and his two squadies, Hunter and Chandler, who had the extra weight of radios and radio batteries and weather kits and fireline handbooks and maps and manifests and extra tools.

Like everyone on the crew, Barnes also carried the fire itself—the weight of his fire shelter, his last piece of protection against being burned; the powdery ash that covered his boots and worked up the insides of his pantlegs to give him black leg; the cuts from tree branches that healed slowly and scarred his wrists; the persistent cough that often turned into bronchitis by September; the retardant slurry that stained the back of his shirt.

And Barnes carried the potential for guilt. His decisions were based on a combination of training and imagination, what the fire was doing and what it might do. And he knew that every decision could carry the weight of a person's soul.

Behind the sawyers and the swampers came Aggie with her lead-P, sighting her handline down the middle of the aerial line cut by the sawyers. Three pulaskis followed her—Kapell, Hassler, and Earl—then George on the first shovel and Warner on another pulaski. If the fire flared up near the front of the line, Aggie would call, "Shovel!" and George and Warner, as the first shovel team, would rush to the front to knock the fire back down. In line behind Warner came three more pulaskis—Horndyke and Freeze, two rookies buried in the line's middle to keep them from trouble, and Stress. The second shovel team followed them—Doobie with the shovel and Lopez with the pulaski. Chandler stayed at the line's tail, pushing everyone along and ready to lead the crew out in case they needed to retreat back down their line.

The line went along like that, with some talking in short flurries of words followed by long silences in which the only noises were the strains of pulaskis and shovels scraping at the ground, the muffled sounds of the chainsaws ahead of the crew, the rushes of the fire like that of a storm moving closer, the disembodied voices on the radios, and the insistent "Bump"—a mantra-like word constantly moving from the line's rear to the front telling each digger to move up as the person behind tied in their piece of line. The line crawled along like an inchworm, stretched out with each person eight to ten feet from the person in front and behind until someone completed that small section of line, three feet wide and down to mineral soil, to the line of the person in front. Then they said "Bump," not too loud for it was only meant to be passed ahead one digger at a time, and then the crew bumped forward another ten feet and dug some more.

Stress, a tall, thin man who ran track at Colorado State during the school year and always boasted about his four-percent body fat, stood once to yell toward the line's front, "Hey. Aren't you guys digging up there? Hell, I'm digging ninety percent of this line. Get your lazy butts in gear."

George answered, "Harness the energy of your mouth and you can dig a hundred percent of the got-damn line."

The second night on the fire, they lit off a two-mile stretch of line, igniting their own fire in short, controlled strips to burn into the main fire. The line between a firefighter and a pyromaniac is as thin as a whistle and Barnes knew everyone on the crew wanted to handle the drip torches, no one more than him. Part of being a crew boss, however, was letting others learn to make the decisions, so Barnes told Chandler to run the fire show.

Chandler smiled, "I'd like Aggie and Freeze to burn with me. Freeze torch the line and Aggie ten yards in and ahead of her. I'll be another ten in. If we need to do any jackpotting, I'll let Barnes know and he'll hold everything up."

The two women nodded. Aggie had burned several times in her years on the crew, but Freeze, a rookie, had never burned before. She watched and copied Aggie as Aggie unscrewed the lid to the drip torch, filled the metal container with fuel, replaced the lid, drained some of the gas-and-diesel mixture onto the grass, lit that with a match, then lit her torch from that fire. Chandler lit his torch and Freeze did also.

"Let's burn, baby," Chandler said.

"Chicks have all the fun," Budd said to Horndyke as they watched Freeze stand in the glow of her drip torch.

"No shit," answered Horndyke.

Twenty yards inside the fireline, Chandler turned and called Barnes to make sure the crew was spread out and ready. Barnes could see the flame of Chandler's drip torch and the man's indefinite outline in its nictating light. He answered that they were set. Chandler held the torch out to his side, a yard of flame arcing from its ignitor wick, and sang, "I am the god of hellfire and I bid you to burn."

Aggie answered with her own song, "I got lightning in my pocket, thunder in my shoes. Have no fear, I have something here I want to show you."

"Yes, ma'am," Chandler cried. "Burn her up."

Freeze smiled excitedly and waited until Aggie had burned a dozen yards before beginning her strip. Only, in her excitement, when Barnes called out for her to go slow and steady, she swung around to answer him and sent an electric arc of flame across the line and into the green.

"Shit-oh-dear," said White. "Freeze is burning the whole damn forest." He stumbled drunkenly over a log to get to the tiny flame Freeze had begun outside their line.

The little spot lasted only a couple of minutes but Freeze's name was added to the Chase Hentzel Award list for the person who committed the biggest screw-up of the season. Doobie had won the previous year for having a fusee ignite in his backpack while taking an extended break too close to the fireline down in Arizona.

The second fire they were on that season, Barnes remembered, was in the River of No Return Wilderness Area in Idaho. They had flown straight out of Redmond from the Oregon fire on the Deschutes National Forest to Boise and then by bus to some small town he could not recall except as through a sleepy haze, then by helicopter into the wilderness area.

The fire's plans chief told him before he boarded the helicopter that more food and water would be packed in by horse and would arrive in two days. They landed in a small meadow of high grasses, unloaded their gear and enough food and water for three days—Barnes knew that the only certainty on a fire is that you can't count on things going as planned.

"Every day's a holiday, every meal's a picnic," Hunter said as the crew set up their spike camp. "Can't beat it. Getting paid to camp out."

"I could have used a shower before we left Redmond," Freeze whined as she filled her water canteens from a five-gallon container left by the helicopter. She had placed her hardhat on the ground and her short blonde hair lay matted and mottled against her head like a plastic wig.

"Quit your bitching, girl," Aggie said. Aggie disliked complainers, and even more, she disliked women who complained. She had been on the Red Feather crew for four seasons, as long as Hunter had been Barnes's lead foreman on the crew, and she knew how others looked at a woman who complained—"a clucking chick" or "on the rag" or "hitting the downside of that PMS curve." It's hard enough, she had once told Barnes, to pull your weight without some rookie girl out of college thinking this is some hike in the woods.

Barnes and Hunter bushwhacked up the hill toward the fire, leaving Chandler to make certain the crew watered up, filled the Dolmars with premix and bar oil, and tooled out with all four chainsaws, ten pulaskis, and four shovels before following the ribbon line left by Hunter to the fire's base.

They had their own ten-acre fire in a complex of fires stretched over miles along the Salmon River, the legacies of a dry thunderstorm that had followed the river's course. That first afternoon and through most of the night, they dug line, encircling the fire inside a rope of dirt before resting for a couple of hours in the early morning. Barnes and Chandler and Hunter took one-hour shifts watching the fire while the crew caught a few winks. The terrain was too steep to sleep on comfortably, so Barnes ended up wrapping himself around a Douglas fir to keep from rolling while he slept. In the morning, after a breakfast of Meals-Ready-to-Eat, Army-issue meals designed for nutrition and weight but not for taste, they improved their line and began mopping up the fire. They spread out to loosely encircle the fire, then searched out every hot spot within ten feet of the fireline. Once certain they had cooled the fire's perimeter, each crewmember began working another ten feet toward the fire's center.

Barnes walked the fire, stopping to help Kapell, a second-year man from Michigan who wanted enough money from that fire season to spend the winter writing poetry in Prague. They took turns working at a deep stump hole, Kapell grubbing with his pulaski and Barnes mixing the hot ash and wood with dirt. He talked with Hunter and Chandler about the crew's condition and how well they had worked the season's first two fires and how the season was off to a good start—good fires, good experience, a pocketful of money waiting back in Fort Collins. He spent time with each of the three rookies, making certain they understood the things they had done over the past days, explaining to Horndyke that he had to work slowly when mopping up, leaving nothing hot that might later jump the line, turning around every so often to be certain of what he had worked, looking at a low angle into the sun for small smokes or hovers of no-see-um insects over hot areas, feeling every piece of wood for heat, grubbing out each stump hole down to cold sand. He helped Sully fell a widow-maker snag that had burned nearly all through. He walked the fire to see everyone and everything.

By evening they had returned to their spike camp at the base of the hill their fire had burned, having left Hunter and half his squad to monitor the fire through the night. They rationed their water and slept. When no food had arrived in the morning, Barnes sent Chandler's squad to relieve Hunter, then he along with Monterey and Ira walked back along a trail to look for the pack train.

A mile back they found an old man dressed in faded and dirty denim and a young woman dressed the same sitting on the trail eating Hostess doughnuts. The ridge there fell off quickly for a hundred feet before dropping off an even steeper cliff to the canyon floor. A hundred yards below in the canyon bottom Barnes could see a black horse, very much dead. Just above the point where the ridge became a cliff lay another horse, also dead. Three other horses stood on shallow benches between Barnes and the nearer dead horse.

Barnes and Monterey and Ira worked their way down to the dead horse a hundred feet below the trail, pulled off its saddle and blanket, and retrieved any food and water containers they could as they climbed back to the trail. The horse had tumbled down the slope and had landed upside down on a branch stob of a large fallen tree. The stob had penetrated the pack and blankets and impaled the horse, probably breaking its back and maybe puncturing a lung. It was a fairly long stob, eight inches or longer, and they worked a good while to roll the horse from it before they could remove the saddle and blanket.

After they walked the three scared horses that had survived the fall back up to the trail, Barnes shared an apple with the woman pack driver. She told him about spending the night on the trail and having to listen to the two dying horses as they cried all night long.

They left that fire the next day after being relieved by a Type-II crew from Utah. "Half-shots and half-shits," Hunter called them as they emptied from the helicopter, their eyes open as wide as their smiles and their fire shirts washhouse clean.

"There but for the grace of God go I," added Stress as he watched the Utah crew mill together like lost sheep.

A hard, insistent knock cowled the morning and withdrew Barnes from his daydream. He answered the front door following the second, even more insistent, knock. In Downey's face, Barnes recognized Max—weathered, angular, lined with years spent in the winters of Montana. He shared the same color blue to his eyes as Max had, clear and hyaline like a glassy sky. He stood just under six foot and still held a textured strength in his body that looked old only in years. His jaw was set. His eyes were leveled straight on Barnes as he opened the screen door without saying anything.

"Barnes," Downey said, flat and unemotional.

"Mr. Downey. Come in."

Downey continued to hold his stare level on Barnes, as a man might contemplate a flat tire.

Barnes held the screen door open until Downey took it and stepped into the house, followed closely by a man Barnes did not recognize. Based on the man's suit and briefcase, Barnes knew his office.

"This is my lawyer, Paul Ginrich," Downey said, indicating the man with him.

Barnes nodded but did not offer his hand, nor did the lawyer offer his. Ginrich dressed in Brooks Brothers and Tony Lamas. Barnes could see the man as someone who drove a truck that never hauled a bale of hay nor touched a road surface other than blacktop, someone who called himself a country lawyer but who never once worked up a callous large enough to split, someone who thought "Skoal" meant a toast over a vodka martini, someone even who actually drank vodka martinis. Barnes took an immediate and intense dislike to the man.

Barnes pointed toward his front room. "We can talk in here," he said. A shade of gray passed across the shadow of his vision. He turned to look briefly into the extra room but did not see anything.

Downey and Ginrich sat at opposite ends of the couch and Barnes sat across from them in a leather chair he had bought at auction over the winter. A woman had shot her abusive husband and then needed to sell their house and furnishings to pay for her defense. After buying the chair, Barnes offered to sell it back to the woman for half what he paid but she declined. "Thank you, no," she said with a sparkle of light bouncing from a tear. "It was his and I don't want it. I need the money more. Thanks anyway. But if you get that quilt over there, I'll do it." Barnes tried, but the wedding ring quilt went beyond his budget.

"You can guess why we're here," Downey said. He sat with his legs spread, feet flat, and his hands stable on his knees. His stare did not waver as he spoke. He pushed his Stetson hat back on his head so that his eyes were not left in shadow.

"I can."

"I want to talk with you man-to-man," Downey said.

"That why you brought him," Barnes nodded toward the lawyer. "He's here—"

The lawyer interrupted Downey. "I'm here because I represent Mr. Downey and his son's legacy. I'm here to make certain that certain things are presented to you so that we all understand where we all stand. I am here to help everyone involved facilitate an understanding that Mr. Downey's son did nothing wrong on that hill and his name should not be denigrated further by any other involved party. I am not here to involve myself nor Mr. Downey in a situation that could become inflammatory."

Barnes felt himself tick another mental notch against Ginrich. He said, "I hope you begin to speak English soon." And regretted the words as soon as he spoke them.

Ginrich smiled a supercilious smile, practiced, Barnes thought, in front of a mirror. Ginrich's face, even through the doughboy puffiness, looked something like a salamander's.

Downey said, "Listen, goddamnit, I'm not here for a pissing match between you two. I want to talk straight with you about my lawsuit against the Forest Service and BLM and about some other people's suits."

"As I told you yesterday and on the phone several times before that, I don't see a good purpose in doing what you're trying to do. I don't think you'll accomplish what you intend to. You may even do more damage to your son."

"Bullshit."

They fell immediately into silence.

"What are you afraid of, Mr. Barnes?" Ginrich asked after allowing the silence to deepen. "If you're afraid that we will somehow try to place all the blame on you, don't be. Our purpose, as I stated at the outset, is to clear Mr. Downey's son of any pall of wrong-doing."

Barnes wished that he could get the lawyer out on a fireline for one day. Give the man a pulaski and start digging. It would either make him a man or put him in a hospital ward crying like a little boy.

"Listen," Mr. Downey said. "We have a copy of a letter you wrote to the parents of Mike Warner. We want you to explain it to us."

Ginrich opened his briefcase and handed over a Xerox copy. Barnes looked at the letter, remembering when he wrote it. Soon after the fire, he had sat down to write letters to the families of each of his people who had died. Each letter began the same, an offer of condolences, followed by memories of the person. Some of these were short, for he had known the three rookies who had died— Freeze, Budd, and Horndyke—for less than twelve weeks before they died. But he recalled some moment that might help a mother understand why her son or daughter would want to do something like fight a wildfire. Some of the letters were pages long, as with Warner's and Chandler's letters. Barnes had met Chandler's family, red-necked white-bread blue-collared ranchers from Julesburg, and he wanted them to know that their son had always been nine-tenths tough as well as one of the best men Barnes had ever known.

He wrote the final part of the letters four times before he sent them. He wanted his account to be the same for each, he wanted no questions that could haunt one family or another. In his first attempt, Barnes had said that nobody could have foreseen what would eventually take place and offered the tragedy as an act of nature. In his next try, he wrote that a series of miscalculations and errors had resulted in the crew being placed in a position from which they could not escape. In the letter he finally sent, he described the fire and, as the crew supervisor, accepted responsibility, and asked the families to contact him if they wanted to know any more.

Barnes could see a slight tremble in his hands as he held the paper loosely. The tips of his fingers became hot and he handed the paper back to Ginrich.

"You say," Ginrich began, then looked down at the paper to quote directly. He began again, a lawyers' trick, Barnes thought. "You say, 'I was responsible for the crew's well-being.' So, you are responsible for what happened."

Downey quickly added, "But that's not exactly what you told the inquisition, the investigating team, is it?"

Barnes took a heavy breath and looked at his hands again. They had steadied. He sat back in the chair and spoke. "What I told the investigation team is what happened. Exactly as I remember it, exactly as it took place."

Both Downey and Ginrich began to speak at once, but Barnes cut them off with a short swing of his hand. "However, I am responsible for my crew. Nobody tells a hot shot crew what to do other than their crew boss. So, yes, in that way I was responsible. I accept that."

"Goddamnit," Downey said, "I knew you'd double-talk this. You tell one group that my son killed these people and then you slide up next to them like a little pup, your tail tucked and your leg lifted in submission. You're a damn coward. Come on. Let's get the hell out of here."

Downey began to stand, but Ginrich placed a hand on his arm and Downey returned to the couch. This time his hands were rolled into fists on his thighs.

Ginrich asked, "What will you say when you have to testify . . . for you will be testifying."

"I will tell the truth."

"And that is?"

"And that is that my crew was my responsibility and that a number of people made wrong decisions on that fire."

"Shit-damn," Downey spat.

"And what will your subordinate, Hunter, your squad leader who lived, say?"

"You'll have to ask him."

"I'm leaving," Downey said. He rose from the couch and this time Ginrich did not try to stop him, neither did the lawyer follow his lead. Downey, the brim of his Stetson curled inside a fist, strode from the room and left the front door open as he left the house. Barnes watched as Downey walked to a rental car parked on the street, slapped the car's top before sitting in the passenger's seat. A haze of false rain clouded the view.

Ginrich stood, as did Barnes.

"This has nothing to do with this case," Ginrich said. "I don't particularly like you."

"Feelings are mutual."

"I have already talked with Hunter as well as some of the smoke-jumpers who were on that fire. They all more or less agree with what you told the investigators. But Downey is a proud man. He loves his son and doesn't want any mark on his family."

"His son did not kill anybody. His son is not to blame for what happened."

"Blame is not the matter, really. It's legacy. And right now, his son doesn't leave the picture he wants."

"A legacy?"

"A hero."

"There weren't any heroes. Max went after that fire as tough as he could. We could have done it better, smarter, but he was a good man."

"But the report implies he did some things wrong."

"The report is right."

"You see. That's not what Downey wants to hear."

"He doesn't want to hear the truth?"

"It's not a matter of truths or lies. It's a matter of perception. And that's why I'm telling you this. If this goes to court, I'll fry your ass. I'll present the perception that, as you say, you are responsible for what took place on that mountain. I'm telling you this so that you can work with us to clear the name of his son."

"You want me to lie."

"No. I want you to present a perception."

Barnes shook his head. "I've got things to do. You can show yourself out."

"Don't fight us on this. You'll lose. You'll lose a lot. I'd rather not take this to court, because there is always the possibility that things could get rather ugly for Downey, turn out bad. I'm going to try and talk him out of this, but if he decides to go forward, I'll be with him one hundred percent. Do you understand? If, in court, you don't help me paint his son in a favorable light, I'll fry your ass. I'll take this letter and hang you with it. All of the bureaucrats and government lawyers together won't be able to keep me from hanging everything about this fire on your head and then I'll hang you."

━━◆━━

Twenty minutes after Downey left, Barnes walked next door to Ruth's house. He thought he could join their morning ritual before Call started Grace to school, lounge for a moment in the love of three generations. Leaving the warmth of his house, Barnes felt a chill from the drizzle outside. The world was so large, he thought, a spiderweb of people and things and emotions. So much so that changes always floated in the air. He thought of how we believe that we live in separate kingdoms, secure and constant, alive with possibilities as old as the land itself. He had discovered, however, that a day turns its corner and suddenly we can live in an exile, fragile and transparent as thin ice.

When on fire assignment, Barnes knew the exact parameters of his world. The actual world existed inside the scraped and charred boundary of the fire for those days or weeks he spent on that fire. Everything else, and everyone else, ceased at the horizon, and the rest of the world became lost for that period of time.

When the fire ended, though, he would return like a forgotten son. As long as the world's scars remained minor, he could look forward to the next fire. Since the previous summer's deaths, however, nothing had remained minor. The sudden exiles, these moments which seemed to have taken lease on his life, these that Barnes had lived through since the middle of the past fire season and which Ruth was now entering, created exclusions for which and from which there seemed no coherency.

Barnes watched a car slow to the stop sign at the street corner which bordered Ruth's house. The car left the intersection, a spray of water ducktailing off the wet blacktop.

As the car's spray filtered down to the blacktop, Tri-pod scurried across the road carrying a black walnut in his mouth. One of

Barnes's favorite moments each morning was seeing that the squirrel had made it through another day of car dodging. Barnes had fed Tri-pod all winter, leaving pecans lining the top of his back fence or walnuts under the elm out front. He knew the other squirrels, those he called Gray-tip and Split-tail, stole their share but he did not care too much. Tri-pod was his favorite—it takes guts, he thought, to be a three-legged squirrel in a world of fast four-wheeled cars.

Barnes watched Tri-pod until the squirrel had climbed an elm and disappeared in its foliage, then he walked the porch stairs to where Ruth stood wrapped inside her own hug. She looked out toward the streams of rainwater in the gutters of the street. He spoke casually, tilting his head toward the front yard, "I think ole' Tri-pod is nesting in the elm."

"Appears to be," Ruth answered without looking up.

"Hope Call doesn't take a notion to start shooting squirrels also."

Ruth smiled. "If he stalks around naked on the porch with that intent, I hope that squirrel harvests his nuts."

Barnes grimaced. "That's not even a comfortable thought."

"Some men could do with a little emasculation."

A pause followed.

"You okay?" he asked.

He did not look straight at Ruth. He looked at the slight rainfall behind her and the squirrel jumping between branches in the old elm. He wanted to keep his thoughts collected and to keep his tone unburnished, but he feared his words carried an emptiness as they both stared at spots in midair.

Ruth finally nodded her head in answer.

Barnes asked, "Where's Grace?"

Ruth lifted her gaze, the first cognizant movement toward

Barnes standing next to her, and Barnes watched her face react to his. He saw a fine woman of lasting beauty not unhappy in her provisional life. Her eyes, as she looked at him, looked empty to him, remnant tears and little recognition. Open windows.

From inside the house, a child's voice called, "I'm here."

"You're here?" Barnes echoed, for the moment glad to leave Ruth's eyes.

Grace opened the front screen and stood with her hands on her hips. A defiant smile crossed her mouth. "I'm here," she repeated with a huff, her chin lifted.

"Hello, 'Here,'" Barnes said.

"Oh, Barnes, you're silly." She stepped back into the house, closing both the screen and the door.

"You have breakfast?" Ruth asked Barnes.

"Coffee straight up," he answered.

"Let's eat, bud. I feel like making someone breakfast and watching him eat it at the table."

"You want to talk?"

"About Robert? Not yet, not just yet. While you're eating and Grace has gone to school, then we can talk."

Ruth poured the remains of her coffee off the porch to mix in her yard with the rain. Raking her fingers through her hair, she turned to enter the house.

Barnes followed. He had sometimes wondered what it would be like to sleep with Ruth, but had always swept the thought from his mind like a sudden change in the weather. She is married, he told himself whenever the thought came, and she has a beautiful daughter and a good father and things are better than good as they are. He told himself not to lose what he already had. In the last months, he had become even better at that, pushing from his thoughts those he wished to keep at a distance. He could not, though, keep the dreams from surfacing at night.

At the dining room table with her arms circled around a bowl of Fruit Loops sat Grace. In front of her was propped a picture book of whales opened to show the tail of an orca slapping the water's surface.

"Hi, Barnes," she said, then looked again at her book.

"Almost done, sweetheart?" Ruth asked her. Ruth stood straighter than she had on the porch and tilted her head up, a mask of strength that Barnes recognized.

"Yes. Why? Why are whales in the ocean?" And she turned to look at Ruth with the question written across her brow, like, Barnes thought, like it was the only thing that mattered then. And maybe, he thought, that was all that should matter.

"Because," Ruth said, then she looked to Barnes for help but he only shrugged. "Because that's the way it is," she said, "because people live in houses and birds fly, I guess."

Grace accepted the answer and finished the rest of her cereal.

Across the table from Grace sat Call, Ruth's father. A slender man with skin baked the color of terra cotta, hair gray and full and flowing over his collar, and an early and slight palsy shaking his hands. He looked as much of a rogue as Barnes had always imagined him being in his youth. Call removed the unlit pipe he kept in the corner of his mouth and greeted Barnes, "How you doing, son?"

"Wet."

"Ain't that the damn truth."

"Daddy." Ruth tilted her head in the direction of Grace, who appeared much more interested in the photographs of her book than in anything any of the adults in the room might say.

Call just smiled and said, "Finish your juice, little darling, because we have to get you to that school of yours. And," he winked at Ruth, "I got me a date for breakfast."

"With whom?" Ruth asked. She had begun to pull jars from her cupboard but stopped to turn back to face Call at the table.

"The 'whom' I'm meeting for breakfast is nobody's business, but I do like your proper English, girl. All that money I spent on college paid off." He winked again, this time at Barnes.

"Daddy, you didn't spend anything on my college. I went to school on scholarships. Your money went elsewhere."

He squinted and shook his head. "Whiskey and women, Barnes. The rest I just squandered away."

"Daddy." Again Ruth tilted her head toward Grace.

"You ready?" Call asked Grace. He placed his pipe back in the corner of his smile where it usually rested, lit or unlit. He fired the pipe only in his study and then only when Grace was asleep upstairs or not home. "My genes," he had said once as he tapped tobacco into the pipe's bowl, "will pass on enough bad habits to that little girl without my environment adding to them."

"Is your date with The Rover?" Ruth asked.

"You're fishing, honey," Call said with a smile. "Since when did I ever call my visits with that old coot a date? But, yes, I'll be meeting him for a game of dominoes later this morning." He added after a calculated moment of silence, "After my date."

"I'm ready," Grace announced. "I want to take something." She thought for a moment. "My whale. My big whale." She pushed herself from the table, climbed off her chair, and put her dishes on the counter in the kitchen. Then she hugged Ruth's legs and Ruth bent down to kiss her. They each said good-bye and Grace skipped from the room.

Call pushed himself from his seat with a slow groan as though he was constructed of rough timbers and rusty hinges. Call and Barnes had shared more than a few bottles of Guinness and fingers of Bushmills when Ruth had left town to join Robert at a literary conference somewhere. The two men would sit with Grace until she went to bed, then one of them would read a couple of stories to her before joining the other for a nightcap on the porch if it was a warm month or in the large leather chairs of Call's study if it was winter. The room smelled of leather and old books and pipe tobacco, a symphony of smells that would quickly place Barnes at ease.

Barnes liked Call, considered him a good man, which, Call had once told him as they both studied the amber shadows thrown from their whiskey glasses, is as good a thing as one man can say about another. They talked often of war and wildfires, loving and losing, restlessness and recklessness.

Barnes had, since moving into the house Call had built years ago for his mother-in-law, considered Call a surrogate for his own father, who had died years earlier without either Barnes or his father ever being able to say they loved the other. Barnes had told Call that, about his father and him, and Call told him that sons and fathers are often too stupid to say what's really important in this world. "Something genetic," he added with a sigh.

As he rose slowly from the table, the old man took a deep breath, smiling as though that might be his last, then limped across the room toward the door. Barnes could see Call in his youth jumping from a hovering helicopter into the neck-deep waters of a swamp in central Vietnam. Call had gone to Vietnam in 1965, a husband and father, a thirty-two-year-old man who believed his cause was good and right. He arrived with the confidence of innocence and left with a handful of medals, a couple of ounces of shrapnel still in his legs and back, and deeper scars he could neither see nor heal. He told Barnes that some nights he still woke with his stomach wrenched and his hands balled into fists at the memory of his war. He told Barnes that some mornings he still woke with the ghosts of men who had died because of his decisions.

Grace skipped back into the kitchen doorway past Call as he left the room and blew kisses at Ruth and Barnes, then she and Call left. The front door shut. To Barnes, it sounded hollow in the echo of the big house.

He sat at the breakfast nook where Call had sat and watched Ruth. She broke two eggs one-handed into a skillet, dropped bread into the toaster, and poured a glass of orange juice. She stood over the stove while the eggs snapped in the hot oil. She twirled her wedding ring and Barnes could see a tear form in her eye. She looked as though she was trying hard to reenter a world from which she had been cast out, a world in which leavings are either innocent or accidental, but seldom desired.

She spatulad the eggs from the pan onto a plate and buttered the toast, but she did not bring them to the table. She stood in a terrible sadness like someone atop a high, cold cornice looking into the yawning of a fogged valley. Barnes watched her gather her strength as she stood rocking slowly against the kitchen counter.

"Everything confuses me." Her words seemed a sigh. With Grace and Call gone, the strength had run from her and even her words were tired.

For a moment there was a stasis in the current of the room. An arithmetic of silence stopped time while Ruth and Barnes looked at each other.

Barnes stood. Ruth lifted her left arm toward Barnes while her right hand traced circles across the linoleum of the kitchen counter. Barnes walked into the embrace of her single arm and then she lifted the other arm and folded it around him. They nestled their faces in each other's neck.

While Barnes ate, Ruth told him the story. She first told Barnes what he already knew, about her meeting Robert while in college and later marrying him, about Call not liking Robert from the first handshake but allowing his daughter to make her own mistakes, about her pregnancy and the birth of Grace, about their years living together in Call's house, about their slow slide away from one another. Barnes understood she needed to tell him everything, like a storm beginning slowly and increasing until it finally blows itself out. The few times she lifted her gaze from the kitchen window to look at Barnes, he could see that her eyes were puffy, red afterthoughts of the passing storm aligned over her clear face.

Barnes ate the breakfast not as much out of hunger, although he was, but from an understanding that Ruth needed to do something for someone else, that she needed to feel needed. So he ate and she talked in a voice almost sinking into a whisper. She would stop occasionally, her feet tapping a slight rhythm on the rug she stood on, as though she had to think for a moment before continuing. Barnes would look up from his plate and see her picking her way through the trails and false starts of her marriage.

Robert, whom she had married when she was almost thirty and stayed married to for over a decade despite his distance, was leaving her, she repeated. He had not yet told her, but she knew. She did not know if he was leaving for another woman or for his career or for both, but she knew he was leaving sometime soon. He no longer touched her when he came to bed, he did not look at her when they passed in the hall, he worked on his papers until she had finished supper before eating his cold. She joked about how he held a book with greater tenderness, but she and Barnes could only force empty laughs.

Ruth talked about how Robert made his living and supported his family with books. He taught literature at the university, had in fact taught some of Barnes's crewmembers over the years. Robert had published little but somehow had brokered an associate professor's position. Still he worked hard at his classes and often spent weekends attending literary conferences with others who liked to talk about Austen or Keats. Barnes had often believed that Robert preferred the life of books to the life of blood. "Books," Call had once offered in discussion, "offer little risk." Call had said to Barnes that he always respected a man who worked hard for his family but not a man who worked long because of his family. After twelve years of his daughter's marriage to Robert, Call still did not like Robert.

In an irony Ruth could not help but smile at, she said that literature was one of the things that had first attracted her to Robert. She was twenty-one and possessed of a wild heart. She liked the sound of beautiful words and thought that a man in possession of those words was also in possession of much more. In time Robert began to live more inside the walls of words and eventually it seemed that all

Robert embraced were those words. They learned how to live with his life and without hers.

Grace, however, became Ruth's second chance, a beautiful, spirited girl of whom even Ruth questioned that Robert could have been the father. Robert, although he loved Grace, was far more comfortable in front of a computer screen than behind a swing.

Ruth told Barnes as he wiped his plate clean with the last of his toast that she had stayed with Robert for the best of reasons—their daughter, Grace—which she conceded was the worst of reasons.

"You know how," Ruth said, "when you're young and you just know that you're meant for something special? Did you feel that way?" She looked at Barnes.

"Yes." Barnes had finished his meal and arranged his knife and fork on the plate. "Everyone wants to be remembered," he said as Ruth poured coffee for them. "To be more than just a flash in the dark."

"Yes." Ruth said the word with a worn surrender. "I feel so tired sometimes, like my heart has rusted over."

She carried the two full cups to the breakfast nook and sat across from Barnes. Barnes could hear the rain outside slapping against the redwood deck off Ruth's house. May, he thought, is supposed to be the month of flowers.

Ruth said, "Sometimes I think that Robert was just a habit I was too blind to see. Not always, not necessarily, a bad habit, but I don't want that monkey back on my back. Somewhere along the line, we became nothing more than comfortable. Is that what it's supposed to be, marriage?"

"You're asking me?"

"No. I guess I'm asking myself. I don't know about guys, but girls, at least the girls I knew in middle school, set a plan in their minds about how their life will be. This will happen and this and this—marriage, or not, and kids, or not. You begin to look at your life like a sweet trip down a golden-hued road. Ken and Barbie in living color. Then all at once I looked in Robert's office at him working on a conference paper on the semiotics of Victorian travel narratives. I see in him an absolutely unknown man there. He was Robert, certainly." She paused for a moment and leaned over with her hands clasped together in front of her on the table. She continued with a con- spiratorial tone to her voice, "I could tell by that little bald spot on the back of his head." She paused again. "But, you know, he was just like an image, vague and bewildered in my mind, that I had plucked out of a poor memory. Right then it was like stepping out of a movie theater into the bright noon sun. Talk about a revelation. Jesus Christ. I sat down and I knew right then that he would leave me because, really, we had left each other quite a long time ago."

Ruth wiped a hand across her face. She drank from her coffee cup and asked if Barnes wanted something more. He answered that he did. She poured him another cup but that was not exactly what he had meant.

"You have Grace," he said slowly.

"I have Grace," she echoed. "She lifts me. She lifts me and she anchors me. She's like a newel post for me."

That evening, Barnes walked the six blocks to a downtown bar. Halfway there, he met a group of college kids walking toward him talking and laughing loudly. They all wore white T-shirts, dark shorts, and baseball caps. The night was too dark for Barnes to see what was written on the shirts and caps, but the kids looked to have on uniforms from how closely matched they appeared. They walked with a swagger as though they owned the sidewalk and Barnes rounded slightly into a yard as they passed. The last of the men, a half-pace behind the others, turned his head toward Barnes, who suddenly felt jacklighted in the temperate shine of a porch light. The kid nodded in silence and Barnes nodded back.

Barnes felt strange, suddenly, to feel them pass into the night behind him, though he had seen people walk those sidewalks on warm evenings for years. He walked very straight, his hands hard inside the pockets of his jeans, and listened and watched the darkness. The kids had walked past like ghosts and Barnes replayed them in his mind as though they were his ghosts.

The ghosts Barnes kept followed the college kids into the night. He smiled unexpectedly, thinking that if Chandler were leading that group of ghosts they would turn and head for the Rio and a round of tequila screamers.

Barnes looked in the large windows of the Rio as he passed, did not see any of his crew. He needed someplace dark where the apparitions were flesh and blood. He rounded a corner and walked down a blind alley to Bake's Back Alley Bar. The small city's real people came to Bake's. There were no ferns, they did not offer grappa as a drink, there were no separate bathrooms. At Bake's, some people played pool, some people played chess, and some people passed out on the bar.

Bake's was darker than the night. Even the lights over the two pool tables looked dark in the haze of cigarette smoke, a haze that had recirculated through the bar for generations.

"Barnes," someone called from a table.

Barnes walked toward the table and found Hunter sitting alone with a beer in front of him.

"Sit down," Hunter said.

Barnes pulled out a chair and sat. Hunter, his assistant on the crew, sat back in the swirl of silence and smoke. The two men seemed to be idling. Barnes felt it and he could tell by the way Hunter waited for him to begin speaking that Hunter also felt their conversation stall until Barnes could place it back in gear.

"Glad I ran into you," Barnes said. And he was, although the thought had not entered his mind until he sat at the table. "Everything going okay at the office?"

"Fine and dandy," Hunter said. While Barnes took a couple of days off before the new fire season began, Hunter took care of last-minute concerns, preparing the crew's cache, testing all of the pumps and chainsaws and video machines they would need over the next two weeks of crew training.

The waitress dropped a coaster on the table and asked, "What can I get you?"

Barnes answered, "Fat Tire."

She wrote on another coaster on her tray. "And you still okay?" she asked Hunter.

"I'll take another."

She turned and left without another word.

"White called," Hunter said. "He wanted to make sure, again, that it was okay that he came back to the crew and to let us know that he's been sober since last year."

Barnes shook his head. "Hell," he said. "It's not his fault that Lopez died. Or maybe it is, but he didn't intend it that way. If he stays sober, then he can stay on the crew. If he sniffs a cork, I'll can his ass real quick."

"I told him as much . . . again. He thinks you probably hate him."

"He's probably right but nobody made me the moral arbiter."

The waitress brought their beers as a man stepped over from the nearest pool table. "These your quarters?" he asked.

"Not mine," said Barnes.

"They're mine," Hunter said to the man. "You play doubles?"

"Only with women and pool." He laughed at his own joke.

Hunter deposited his quarters for the balls and racked them. Barnes remained sitting, watching his friend arrange the table for a game of eight ball. The other guy, large and sweaty, looking like he slept in Bake's, lined the cue ball for his opening strike. The man's head was shaped like a cuesta hill, a gentle slope up the greasy backside of his hair and a quick, flat face. A head that had been shaped by a fast-moving glacier or by too many brawls.

"Nickel a ball?" the man asked.

"Five bucks it is," Hunter said. "It's your paycheck."

The man snapped his cue stick and the balls collided, sending the table into a kaleidoscope of motion. The immediate and violent anarchy of the break slowed into a disharmony of sixteen scattered balls on the table and none in the pockets.

"Shit," the man said. "Your shot," he added as he walked to a table, his belly leading the way.

Hunter chalked a cue as he paced around the table, stopping to study an angle before pacing back to where he first stood.

"You going to shoot?" yelled the man with the cuesta head. His friend, almost as large, sat slouched in his chair, watching Hunter.

"You can't rush greatness," Hunter said without looking at the two men sitting in the fulsome darkness away from the table.

"You just got to," Hunter began as he leaned over the table and shot the ball into the side pocket, "watch and admire." Hunter downed two more balls before missing a bank shot on the four ball.

Cuesta said to his friend, "Get some, bro."

Bro nodded. He did not look drunk until he staggered to the table, and then he lost his drunkenness as soon as he reached the table. Like a man crossing ice, he reached the other side and found his legs. He did not find, however, a shot, for Hunter had left him boxed in against the rail.

"That's a piss-poor lay," Bro said.

"That's what she said," added Cuesta. He laughed alone.

Bro lined a shot he hoped would leave Barnes as stuck as him. Barnes stood and took Hunter's cue stick. He leaned against the wall next to the rack of cues.

Cuesta joined him. The man smelled rancid from beer and sweat and cigarettes. Before Barnes could move away, Cuesta said, "That buddy of yours sure is cocky."

Barnes did not answer. He looked at Cuesta's face, four days removed from a razor and red like an alcoholic's.

Cuesta added, "He any good at this?"

"Not bad," Barnes said as Bro banked the cue ball in an effort to hide it in the top corner behind the ten ball. He hit it too hard and the cue ball bounced into the open.

"Your shot, man," Cuesta said.

Barnes looked over his choices. He had only one shot with the seven ball a sitting duck in the far side pocket, but he took his time just the same.

"Damn, man. You guys always take this much time?" Cuesta asked.

"Only with women and pool," Hunter answered.

Cuesta spat on the bar's floor and glared at Hunter. Bro handed him another bottle of Budweiser and Cuesta wrapped his lips around the end like a sucker fish.

Barnes considered downing the eight ball and ending the game right then.

Hunter walked to Barnes and whispered, "You feeling tough tonight?"

Barnes answered, "I hope we won't find out."

"I think it's so." Hunter slapped Barnes on the shoulder and walked back to their table. He did not sit, though, and kept his eyes on Cuesta and Bro.

Hunter was not large, just over six foot and of medium build, about the size of most firefighters. Too small and the long hours and longer hikes wore a firefighter down, too large and the hours spent bending over a pulaski took too heavy a toll on the back. Hunter ran and worked out every day on weights, both for vanity and his job. His black hair was cut short as it was every year, once a year at the beginning of the fire season. Hunter liked to play the harmonica and did not mind an occasional fight, especially after he had a few beers to prime his pump.

Barnes pocketed the seven and left himself a shot at the two ball. He downed that but went no further.

Cuesta walked to the table and stood there, his hand on his chin, pretending to study the table. "This how they do it, bro?"

"Looks like it," Bro answered.

"Hell, man. Quick and dirty is what I say. Just scream shit and shoot."

Bro laughed, sounding more from habit than actual enjoyment. "With women and pool," he said and laughed again.

"Let me see. We got the spots?" Cuesta asked.

"Like hell," Hunter replied. "You got stripes. Should be enough of them on the table to make it easy on you."

"Fuck that, man," Cuesta said. He knocked the twelve ball in, then the eleven, then the thirteen, but missed a long straight shot across a yard of green at the fifteen.

Cuesta bumped shoulders with Hunter as they passed each other. Neither turned to look at the other, but Barnes could see Hunter's smile. The table laid out with the solid balls all hovering near pockets. With a little luck, Hunter would look like a shark.

Barnes stood with his back to the wall and watched Hunter begin his run. Halfway through the run, Cuesta walked over and asked Barnes, "Did he sucker me?"

"You offered the bet. He just agreed."

"A little too quick I think."

"No matter. It's just a friendly game."

"My ass. We'll play double or nothing on the next one."

"He's just getting warmed up. You might consider quitting while you're ahead," Barnes said.

"Fuck that shit, man."

By then, Hunter had deposited all the solids and banked the eight ball into the corner pocket. He leaned on his pool cue while Cuesta pulled a twenty-dollar bill from his wallet and tossed it on the table.

Cuesta bent to rack the balls for the next game. His white T-shirt pulled up on his back and his jeans lowered as he leaned over, exposing the crack of his butt.

Hunter murmured to Barnes, "That plumber's smile gets any bigger and he'll have to take out a union card."

With the balls racked, Hunter broke and dropped two solids into pockets. "A place for everything, and everything in its place," he said as he paced the table searching out his next shot.

"Shit," Cuesta said and walked to his table, leaving Barnes and Bro standing next to each other against the wall. The Texas Tornadoes were on the jukebox singing "Que Paso."

"My buddy's not having a good time," Bro said after a drink of beer.

"Doesn't look like it."

"He don't like to lose, man."

"It's only a pool game. It's not life or death."

"He's not a good loser. Don't matter if it's having to stop at a stop sign, he don't like it."

"I'm afraid he'll probably lose big time."

Bro continued talking as though Barnes had said nothing. "His wife's a pig"—Barnes did not answer that the man was not exactly buffed beefcake himself—"he hates his job and now he gets his ass kicked at pool. Shit-for-damn." Bro shook his head, then pulled hard on his Bud. "You work in Fort Collins?"

"The Forest Service."

"No shit? Like a forest ranger or something?"

"We fight forest fires."

"No shit. You and him fight forest fires? Like that one killed all those dudes last year?"

"Like that."

"You know any of them?"

"Who?"

"Those guys got killed."

"Yes, I knew them."

"Sounded pretty bad, man."

"Yes."

"Chicks and all. Man."

"Yes."

"You knew them, huh?"

"Yes."

"You weren't there, were you?"

"I was there."

"No shit, man. How'd you live?"

"I don't know."

"Lucky, I guess."

"Yes. Lucky, I guess."

"How'd you know them?"

"I was their crew boss."

"You were their boss?"

Hunter's run ended with only one solid ball left on the table's green. He winked at Barnes as he walked to their table for another beer brought by the waitress.

Bro sidetracked on his way to the table and talked with Cuesta. He motioned toward Barnes as he talked with the big man, who grabbed his beer and joined Barnes standing near the wall. Cuesta had a menacing smile spread across his face as he approached Barnes. Before speaking, he waited for Bro to sink his first ball and leave himself in line for a decent run.

Cuesta said, "So you guys killed all those dudes over there near Craig." It was not even close to a question.

Barnes shook his head and began to walk away.

"Damned chicken-shit coward," Cuesta said loudly. The bar skipped a beat. The jukebox stopped just then and so did everyone and everything else in the bar. The bronchitic breathing of the patrons formed all the sound other than the swish of a pool cue cutting the cigarette haze.

Cuesta did not even have time to raise his hands as Barnes turned and swung his pool cue. The cue left a wake of silence in the haze before it connected solid against the side of Cuesta's meaty neck. Barnes followed the cue with a punch to the man's solar plexus, or at least to the area that should have been his solar plexus.

Everything happened quickly then. Bro punched Barnes between the shoulder blades but Hunter took out Bro with a punch that sounded as though it broke the man's nose. The exhilarating sound of fist hitting bone suffused the room and seemed to fill Cuesta with a rage. His face broad and red, Cuesta came toward Barnes with a roll of his shoulders, looking like a boxer off the opening bell. Barnes weaved to the side. A smash to the cheek, hooks and haymakers, jolts to the face. Cuesta hit and Barnes hit back, connecting against the man's face and shoulders. The fight ended as quickly as it began with bouncers and bartenders separating the men, sending Cuesta and Bro out the main door and Barnes and Hunter out the kitchen.

Along College Avenue, groups of college students and high school kids loitered in the warm summer evening. An inversion had all but dried away the day's rain. The high school kids stood in huddles on the street benches waiting for a cruiser they knew to drive by. Horns honked, waves flashed as did signs, yells died in the hum of truck tires. The college students talked, watched the cruisers drive by, drifted in and out of crowded bars. None of them, not the students nor the kids, carried any sense of tomorrow much less of mortality.

Barnes and Hunter crossed their paths and passed their groups almost without being noticed. They walked to a café and sat across from each other at a booth. Barnes could feel a bruise rising on his cheek and his hands had already swelled.

"You guys been having fun tonight?" the waitress asked.

"Does it look like it?" Hunter laughed. He had not been hit in the quick fight, having dropped Bro with his one punch before the bouncers intervened.

"You don't look so bad," she said. "But your friend, here, looks like he tried kissing a truck."

"Sometimes you're the bug and sometimes you're the windshield," Hunter said.

The waitress laughed her customer laugh. "What can I get you?"

"Coffee for now," Hunter answered.

The waitress walked away.

"Nice ass," Hunter said.

"I'm forty-five. I'm too old for that shit," Barnes said.

"What?"

"The fight."

A northbound Greyhound droned by on the road outside, the shadows of the riders just shades on the darkened windows. A police siren erupted in inscrutable wails as it headed east.

Barnes could feel his head beginning to throb. "We could have ended our fire season a week before it began."

"We could have, but we didn't. And we didn't get our asses kicked."

"It was still stupid."

"Maybe, but didn't it feel good?"

Barnes looked at Hunter. His head was definitely throbbing, his hands could not hold the coffee cup the waitress had just filled, and the welt under his eye had ballooned into a baseball.

"Well, maybe you don't feel all that good physically, but it had to have been cathartic—smacking that sonofabitch. Haven't you wanted to hit someone since the fire? A reporter who doesn't know shit about forest fires but passes some judgment anyway, that asshole lawyer getting ready to sue your ass, White, Max Downey, Chandler, yourself. Somebody?"

Barnes tried breathing hard, but he must have taken a punch to the chest and the storage area in his lungs had been reduced. He patted the sore spot on his cheek and felt its tenderness and warmth extending around his eye. "It did. It was still stupid, but, man, I could see a handful of faces I've wanted to hit all flash in front of me when I punched that big bastard. If he weren't so damn big and tough, I'd have killed him."

"At least you got to do something," Hunter said, grave and convinced.

Barnes nodded in agreement, feeling that some small amount of the frustrations of will he had fought for months had been lifted. Nothing had changed. A dozen of his people had still died, a handful of families had or would name him as a related party in lawsuits, many more people still thought him a coward of some kind. He had felt himself sliding into an inevitable weakness. Hitting Cuesta was hitting a lot of people.

He also felt an embarrassment that he needed to hit someone to make himself feel better and tried reconciling that in his mind, which through the throbbing was having enough difficulty just focusing on the coffee cup in front of him.

"Downey's father and his lawyer stopped by my house today after work," Hunter said. "He implied that if I help him out in court my name will only be mentioned in favorable terms. His implication was that if I don't help him, I'll be cast poorly. I could have kicked his ass."

"Downey's only trying to save his son."

"By ruining others."

"He doesn't see it that way."

"I told him. I told him what happened. I told him that his son didn't kill anyone, but actions have results. It was, ultimately, Max's decision to dig that line. I told him that, but he wouldn't listen to any of it."

"I think his lawyer has tried."

"He didn't try while I was there."

"He's supporting his client."

Hunter snorted, "He's an asshole, a bottom-feeding fish. He doesn't know and he doesn't care, just so long as he makes his roll and walks out of the courthouse clean and well-pressed."

"Asshole."

"Asshole."

"You eating?" Barnes asked.

"No. I need some serious sack time. You need a ride home?"

Barnes told Hunter that he would walk home to clear the mind and stretch the already aching muscles. He took a warm shower after he got home. His body had stove up tight, and he could see in the shower's shaving mirror that his eye would swell but not discolor. After the shower, he lay in bed and drifted in his loss. He fell asleep to the hushed sounds of shadows moving across the wood floors of his house.

Chapter Three

WEDNESDAY

O nly his ghosts stood in the room. They had lined themselves along the far wall and watched silently as Barnes studied each of their faces. Barnes stood tense and motionless except for the movement of his eyes and his head. His tension loosened when he came to Horndyke's face with the almost-dumb smile.

They had returned from the Idaho fires the previous summer looking forward to a couple of days off. A couple of days to reattach themselves to lovers and friends and children. Run a load of wash, shower two or three times, and shampoo once more to scrub the last few weeks of fire from their bodies. Eat a meal with friends and be able to enjoy the taste and not simply consume the food. Pay the overdue bills and clean the refrigerator of soured milk and composted vegetables. In White's case, come to find his girlfriend had cleaned out the joint bank account and had split to Los Angeles with her previous boyfriend. Or in Hunter's case, come home to find that his wife, unable to withstand the temptation of a single three-thousand-dollar check floating softly inside the grasp of her fingers, had bought a new Ford Thunderbird.

Most slept on the plane ride home and almost all slept on the bus ride from the airport south of town. They unloaded all of their gear, gathered for a short discussion between Barnes and Chandler and Hunter about the crew's performance in Idaho, refilled their water bottles in case they were called out in the night, exchanged worn tool files and head lamps and gloves for new ones, and left for the showers and a beer or ten. The sawyers stayed for an extra hour to strip and clean their Stihls. They cleaned the tracks of their bars with the cutting edge of P-38 can openers and blew the housings dry with an air hose, exchanged their worn files for new ones, and replaced the chains and spark plugs and air filters on their saws. Then they also left the crew's cache and compound a couple blocks from the university for home or the bars.

Many of them met that evening at the Rio for margaritas and Mexican beer. Barnes walked in about seven o'clock thinking much of his crew would be there and having something of note to tell them. He heard a shout as he opened the restaurant's door, Chandler's shout following a tequila screamer, what Chandler named a Jose Cuervo hooker chased with a cathartic yell. The usual din momentarily ceased in the bar except for Freddie Fender singing "Wasted Days and Wasted Nights" over the stereo system. The yell's echoing waves subsided and people returned to their drinks and conversations. Barnes weaved his way between college girls in tight skirts and fraternity boys in muscle shirts toward the scream's epicenter.

Chandler, Aggie, Kapell, Ira, and Horndyke stood hunched over the far end of the tiled counter that divided the bar in half. Five empty shot glasses and five bottles of beer in various states of emptiness and a scavenged platter of chicken nachos scattered the counter in front of them.

Aggie saw Barnes first. She waved. "Barnes, you rutting around with the grunts tonight?" She pulled an empty stool next to her for Barnes to sit on.

"Just a couple of beers to drown the Idaho dust."

"A Sol, right?" Chandler asked and waved down a waitress. "A Sol and a shot for my friend."

"As long as I don't have to listen to another scream," the waitress answered.

"From Barnes?"

"From anyone."

"Just cutting loose a little, sweetheart."

The waitress leveled her eyes. "Don't sweetheart me, Chandler."

"Okay. No screamers, unless of course you're free after your shift."

"Chandler, you're lucky you're cute," the waitress said.

"Oh, darling, you're making me blush."

"Shut up and order."

"A Sol for my friend."

"And another round here," Horndyke added.

"Of shots or beer?" the waitress asked.

"Beer," said Aggie.

"And shots," added Horndyke. He wore his lucky T-shirt, BALL-U printed across its front. He was a forestry student at Ball State in Indiana.

Horndyke was the only one besides Barnes not wearing a crew T-shirt—cream colored with a red feather on the left breast and RED FEATHER HOT SHOTS printed in an arc above it. Another feather caught in the blaze of a flame stretched across the shoulder blades of the shirt's back with the single word FIRE stenciled beneath. Barnes wore a white button-down shirt and, like the rest of them, Levi's. He only wore his crew T-shirt on duty.

Chandler had pushed the sleeves of his T-shirt up on his biceps, as he tended to do when he became serious in his drinking. On his right arm, he wore a thinning tattoo of a poker hand, aces and eights.

"How many shots you guys have?" Barnes asked.

"One," Kapell answered. "Two for Chandler. He's figuring he may need tequila goggles tonight. Beer goggles just won't do it." He pointed toward a couple of women sitting nearby with hair a couple of stories high and denim dresses a couple sizes too small. The combination made them look as though their dresses had squeezed their bodies up through their hair. The amount of make-up they wore made it nearly impossible to tell exactly how they looked, but, as Kapell whispered confidentially, "Those two are long on ugly."

"The man's a pig," Aggie said, shaking her head.

Kapell looked at her as though she had meant him.

"Yeah, you too," she said.

"Just be thankful he ain't studying you," Kapell laughed. He nudged Aggie with his elbow, but not hard because Aggie stood his height and carried his weight and packed a much meaner punch.

"If he were studying me," she answered, "that would be the last book he'd ever open." Aggie drank from her beer. She could match any man other than Chandler at twelve-ounce curls, as the rookies all found out during the crew's end-of-training party in May.

"They're beginning to look awful nice," Chandler said. "Just a few more and they'll look like my dreams."

"Slut," Aggie said.

"Can't deny it," Chandler said. "I'm sleeping in some sweet

baby's arms tonight," he added and lifted his glass over the counter between them.

Kapell raised his glass to meet Chandler's and said, "Here's to the Red Feather, those hardy sons of bitches. They wipe their ass with broken glass and laugh because it itches."

Barnes smiled as the five drank the rest of their beers.

The waitress put the refills on the counter. "To your tab, Chandler?" she asked.

"Hell, yes," he said. "I had a good day at the office, honey. And if these guys don't pay me back, I'll work it out of them in sweat and tears."

Ira, not the most experienced person on the crew but still the oldest besides Barnes, nodded toward Barnes, "I'm not so certain us old boys can keep up." He tipped his bottle toward Barnes.

"I'm not so certain this old boy wants to," Barnes answered and met Ira's bottle top with his own.

"It's going to be a good night, Barnes," Horndyke said, wearing the smile Barnes swore signaled the man was a couple of Milk Duds short of an entire box. Horndyke's eyes hid under the shadow of his ballcap and behind the round of his reddened cheeks. He added, "Budd and Doobie and Dago are coming down later."

"I wouldn't go too hard," Barnes said.

"Why's that?" Chandler asked. His tone dropped a notch into the serious. He had been with Barnes for four years, two as a squad foreman, and recognized certain signs in Barnes's voice.

Barnes sipped his beer, then placed it back on the tiled counter. He wiped his mouth and wished that he had time for a couple more bottles. "I talked with dispatch a half-hour ago," he said. "Eastern Washington has a red flag warning posted, five good fires already in Chelan and the Entiat Valley and dry lightning hitting the area again tonight. She said from what she's heard that we can expect a call."

"Ka-ching, ka-ching," Aggie said. "I hear my bank account registering big bucks."

"I knew we'd hit a thousand hours again this year," Kapell said. "What do we have now?"

"More than two hundred," said Chandler. "So we'll hit a thousand overtime easy if Southern Cal burns this fall."

"Keep 'em coming. Papa needs a brand new car."

"Don't get ahead of things," Barnes said evenly. "Let's just take what we get and enjoy the trip."

"Damn," said Horndyke, pushing the ballcap up on his forehead. He frowned and held the amber bottle of Negro Modelo beer between his hands. "I kind of wanted a party night. I was feeling lucky tonight."

"Give me a break," Aggie said.

Barnes shook his head. "I'd finish these and hit the sack," he said, then drank from his beer but left the tequila alone.

"Hell, Barnes, I just came out here for a little fun," Horndyke said.

"I don't take drunks on fires." He spoke firmly but with a smile. He understood how enjoyable a night out after twenty days spent on fires could be. He had counted the flight between the Oregon and Idaho fires as a day of paid rest and when asked about how fresh his crew was he reported them rested and well.

"Yes, boss," said Kapell in a minstrel voice.

Horndyke pouted a little more, then said, "I guess this just means we'll have more money for next time."

"I'm getting something to eat, then heading home," said Kapell.

"Oh, hell," said Aggie. "You can eat in November."

"And sleep when you're dead," Chandler added.

Barnes left them then. He had hoped to find Lopez with them. She usually joined Aggie for beers at the Rio. They formed anti-thetical images when they entered a bar together. Aggie had swimmer's shoulders as wide as a man's and arms and thighs heavily muscled. She stood as tall as most men and wore her ash-colored hair down when not on a fire. She looked like an Amazon standing next to Lopez, who was small with soft brown skin and long black hair, turbid eyes, and a soft mouth that smiled.

Barnes had not had the opportunity to be alone with Lopez since the season had begun to roll. He wished he could have spent some time with her that night.

The dispatcher's telephone call came a few hours later, after Barnes had fallen asleep, dreaming of the set of almond-shaped eyes and the slow curve of the mouth, the soft illusions which formed the parts of her face. He woke quickly and completely and sat on the edge of his bed to answer the phone. He kept a pad of paper and pencil next to the phone and his fingers automatically picked up the pencil.

In a faint and low undertone, Barnes repeated the dispatcher's words as he transcribed them: "Wenatchee National Forest. . . . Entiat Valley Complex. . . . Probably Oklahoma Gulch Fire. How large?" He clicked his pencil for more lead. "Two hundred acres and running in brush and pine and spotting. . . . Loveland–Fort Collins Airport at 4 A.M."

He read the information back to the dispatcher and thanked her for calling. He wrote down the time—1:12—from the luminescent numbers on his clock.

"Hot-damn," he said aloud.

Before showering he called Hunter and Chandler. He also called the pager service. That completed the root habit following a fire call, the objective business that formed the first few minutes.

A rush of adrenaline, wholly expected and welcomed, punctured his initially prosaic and methodical reaction and pulsed through him as he stood under the shower's spray. He soaped his body quickly and rinsed, standing with his hands against the wall of the shower on either side of the shower head and letting the stream of water rain on him. He felt his body running like its choke had stuck open.

Barnes loved his job. He loved fighting wildfires. Everything about it. The camaraderie of a hot shot crew, the adrenaline rush and the risk of tragedy, the long hours with his head in the dust and the dirt and smoke, the knowledge that a banker or a politician or a college professor could not do this and survive the first day, the end of the day and standing on a ridgetop and watching the fire creep or run toward you and your line and seeing that fire stopped then by what you did.

As much as fighting a wildfire, Barnes liked the anticipation of one. Once on the fire, often things would again level out—the size-up, the attack, the mop-up. Every fire had its own personality and its own rhythm, but they seldom matched the sudden jolt from routine that immediately followed a dispatch. The world suddenly shrank in size and transformed with its center inside a fire's flame.

Barnes finished the shower, looked over his gear one last time to make certain he had repacked everything in his war bag. He checked the crew manifests. His world again slid into the ordinary of recurrent preparations. The adrenaline would return once he saw the smoke column rising into the air as a pillared stain against the sky.

By the time Barnes had driven from his home across town to the cache, Hunter had already arrived and was seated at Barnes's desk taking telephone calls. Hunter sat back in the chair and crossed his feet on top of Barnes's desk. He wore green Nomex fire pants and his crew T-shirt, and his White's boots hung unlaced. His red war bag braced the wall next to the desk alongside his line pack, his hardhat and yellow fire shirt stacked on top. The coffee pot grumbled across the room on Chandler's desk with Stress and George seated nearby, empty cups in their hands and their heads dropped to their chests.

Barnes nodded toward Stress and George after he leaned his briefcase against the desk.

"Just tired," Hunter said. "Stress said he'd just started taking off his pants when the pager went off. They'll be fresh when we land."

"They don't have a choice."

Barnes leaned forward to look at the roster sheet. All of the names had checks next to them except Lopez. "Lo-girl not call in?"

"No."

"You call her at home?"

"Just now. Not there."

Barnes sighed. He took his coffee cup over to Chandler's desk to wait with Stress and George for a moment.

Within minutes the crew began straggling in, none of them anywhere near bright-eyed and bushy-tailed, but none of them falling-down-drunk. Warner walked into the cache office, his eyes blinking awake. He stumbled toward the coffee maker like an old man looking for his spectacles.

White tripped over his own bootlaces as he entered the room. "That bitch," he slurred.

"What now?" asked Hunter.

"She took all my money and split to California."

"What the hell you talking about?"

"While we was in Idaho, she emptied the bank account and split on me."

Barnes asked, "You had a joint account with your girlfriend of, how long, a month?"

"Yeh."

Hunter said, "Does the word stupid mean anything to you?"

"Oh, man, I need a lawyer."

"You need a good fire so you can pay for a lawyer."

Ira called from the coffee pot, "What you need now, son, is coffee. Come and partake in this delight. A robust yet mellow bean."

Everyone in the room stopped what they were doing and stared at Ira.

"Sorry," he said. "I got carried away with the moment."

Chandler was next to enter the harsh glare of the office's fluorescent. He stood in the doorway squinting and rubbing his face with both hands.

Hunter laughed, "Rode hard?"

"Not even," Chandler answered, "but I was sure-as-shit put away wet."

Barnes said to Chandler, "Make certain the saws are purged and loaded. Let's take one falling saw with us and extra bars and chains for the others."

"Monterey's right behind me," Chandler said. "He's the saw boss, he'll take care of it. Right now I can't do any heavy lifting."

None of the people in the room said anything. They looked first at Barnes and then closely at Chandler still standing in the doorway, his legs spread wide.

"At this moment," Chandler said with a disordered smile, "if it's heavier than a cup of coffee or a can of beer, I can't lift it."

Dago held a full cup of coffee toward Chandler. "Here you go, big guy."

Chandler took it and drank the cup down. "Jesus, that's shitty coffee. Let me make some real-man's coffee for you pups. You need something with attitude to jump-start these lazy-ass motors."

"It's not just a job, it's an adventure," Monterey said as he pushed past Chandler. "Fill me a cup of that attitude when it's right," he said to Sully, who stood with the others near the coffee pot watching Chandler dump handfuls of coffee into the maker's top.

Monterey said to Barnes, "I'll pull out the bars and chains and see they make it into the saw bag. Sully, you can purge the saws."

Behind Monterey walked Budd and Lopez. Budd had a smile across his face, and he winked toward Horndyke as he entered the cache office. Lopez ignored Barnes.

The flight to Washington was straight and simple. The only sounds were snores and whispers. They landed in Wenatchee and boarded a Greyhound bus for the forty-five-minute drive along the Columbia River to base camp. While Barnes checked in at the plans tent, the crew filled their water bottles then ate breakfast. After a short briefing, they tooled out and waited at the heliport for their helicopter flights to a spike camp near the Oklahoma Gulch Fire.

With the ghosts of his crew fading before him into the morning's new light, Barnes felt as though he danced through his mornings with these ghosts, always in step and never tripping, yet also never embracing in their slow sunlit waltz. He wanted to reach out for them and take them in. For a long while after the fire, he wanted to be one of them and sometimes he still thought he should be.

In the hours following the ghosts' departure, he would catch his balance, sometimes quickly and sometimes gradually in broad degrees. Sometimes he felt as though he fell off balance. No issues had resolved and a morning would push on toward afternoon in a nervous jag. That Wednesday, though, the day moved in the slow waltz left from the dance with his spirits. His ghosts had left, but in their leaving a shaded presence remained that accompanied Barnes through the day. They were with him over the newspaper and yet another article on the tragedy fire of the previous season, and then at the long stoplights along College Avenue, in the stores and on the concrete sidewalks and brick walkways of downtown, at home as he wrote letters, and with him again while he sat on his porch with the afternoon sun still hours from falling behind the Front Range.

Earlier, soon after lunch, he got a phone call from the father of Max Downey. Downey's voice rose like a violent sun, hard and inflexible as he confronted Barnes. He threw the same questions at Barnes—"Tell me what happened," he would always ask, but the question was joined by an assaulting plea to not indict his son. "Will you testify in court?" he would ask. "But only tell the truth I want to hear," he would leave unsaid. And again Barnes told Downey that he saw no reason to go to court.

Downey's voice tightened, "You don't give a shit, do you?"

"A lot of people made mistakes. Your son included," Barnes sighed flatly.

He absently traced across the unfolded pile of washed clothes littering his bed. He looked up and searched his room for some definite illumination, something to hold with his mind.

He found the necklace Lopez wore, a rosary of wooden beads from which she had removed the cross. He could see her as the pyric fire burned over her, in the second between when she knew she would die and when she did die. He could see her hand reach instinctively for the loop of metal links joining the wood beads smaller even than piñon nuts. Her fingers searching in vain for the relic of her religion in that single lustrum second. And then only her, curled into herself on the empty and swept fane of the hillside.

Barnes trailed the short length of the rosary where it hung on a supporting post for his mirror, where Lopez had placed it the last night she had slept with him. He had thought of returning it to her in the days following that night as last year's crew gathered for their two weeks of training. He had thought of returning it but he had not. It remained with him as some people keep a song's melody in their ear. He kept it and she had burned without it and now he kept it with a sense of shadowy dependence.

"You son of a bitch." Downey's words damned him. "You're still alive and you don't care about them, do you? You son of a bitch."

An expanding, frozen silence wedged between them. Barnes could feel his ghosts hovering, listening over his shoulder. Their presence cooled the room and Barnes closed his body. On the other end of the telephone, Downey waited with his own ghost. Barnes felt the other man attempting to reach inside him and draw from him some enclosed fiber. Barnes felt the man's furious pull as he listened to the incentive breathing of Downey.

Finally Downey spoke again, his voice less commanding but more condemning, "You weren't even there last weekend. We thought we'd see you then, at the commemoration of the trail, but you're so damned gutless you wouldn't even show for that. You haven't been back, have you?"

"This isn't getting us anywhere. I've told you I can't help you."

"My wife lost her youngest son. You are a bastard, you know that? My boy died up there and people think he caused all those deaths." His voice broke and suddenly another voice replaced it, a more tired and defeated voice of the same man. "Is it that easy for you? Knowing that a dozen of your crew burned along with my boy. Have you found it that easy to let go?"

Barnes said nothing.

"You really haven't been back, have you?" demanded Downey.

Barnes clenched his eyes tight to remove any trace of image or memory behind the violent orange-black of his closed eyelids. His free hand balled into a fist and if he had had someone to hit he would have, but instead he shook with the tension of his muscles. He said slowly and deliberately, "What the hell do you want me to say, Mr. Downey? Your son was the IC. He decided on the plan of attack and took half my crew into that canyon. They all died. They died because a lot of people made wrong decisions and because the fire and the weather and the land all conspired against us, but we did it wrong. Me and your son and others. We did it wrong."

"You're a bastard," Downey said and hung up.

Barnes stood in a whirlwind, thoughts cascading around him with a spinning gyre. He thought of the lowest cross, Chandler's cross, the cross farthest from the safety of the ridgetop. A white concrete cross maybe two feet into the air, just as high as the top of his knee. WALKER CHANDLER engraved in bold script across the horizon of the cross. RED FEATHER HOT SHOTS engraved below that. From Chandler's cross, Barnes could see the other thirteen crosses, the eleven of his crew, and those for Max Downey and Russell Fleming, the smokejumpers. He could see the ragged trail of crosses like a horrible connect-the-dots pattern in the gray dirt of the hill. He could see where Dago and Sully died together, Dago possibly trying to crawl under the deployed fire shelter Sully had prayed would save his life but did not. Other groups of two or three crosses marking the bodies. And there alone, the cross for Lopez, a half-dozen feet from anyone else's cross. The crosses stood as an unbreachable boundary between here and there, an impossible counterpoint.

Impaled by the ghosts of those cement crosses, Barnes spent the whole of that Wednesday afternoon watching a broken memory where they died in fetal curls, perished in their youth and hugging their earth for protection.

Lopsided slants of waning sunlight spread across the bedroom. Sometime during the afternoon, following the height of his mind storm, he realized that he had lain out across the length of one of those slants of light on the hardwood floor of his front room. He had been shaking but had warmed himself in the sun.

He wanted something simple. He boiled water and brewed a cup of tea, twisting and straining the tea bag around a spoon, then cupping the warm tea bag in his hands and holding it close to his mouth and nose to embrace the warmth of the scented steam rising from it. He drank that cup of tea, then mowed his lawn and changed the oil in his truck and turned his compost pile. He brewed another cup of tea to wait out the day in the sun of his porch.

Barnes sat holding the cup of tea on his leg. Again, the telephone rang inside his house but Barnes let the machine answer. He heard a voice talking but did not care to listen. The spring sunshine felt pleasant and the chatter of Tri-pod from the lower branches of an American elm held his attention. He grew sleepy in the sun. He placed the tea on the wood floor of the porch and extended his legs, folding his arms across his chest and resting his head against the wall behind him. He slipped leisurely to the edge of sleep until Call brought Grace home from kindergarten.

Call, dressed in denim shirt and Levi's and wearing a worn Stetson, waved to Barnes as though waving away smoke.

Barnes's hand paused before returning the wave. He watched across the connected yards, separated only by a waist-high fence with strands of ivy winding up and around the posts and boards. A silence held around Barnes for a minute as he watched Call walk deliberately around the car's front to help Grace from her seat. Call stood tall and straight and broad-shouldered, but his movements were slowed with the wounds of war and age, and he used the car as a cane when he unbent.

The silence which hovered around Barnes like a sheltered pocket broke with Grace's young voice. "Barnes," she called and waved and ran.

Barnes sat up and stretched but he did not leave his seat. He watched Grace run from the car parked at the curb, along the sidewalk, jumping across the cracks, and then turning for the last dozen feet and up the stairs to where he sat. He felt a sudden rush of panic as he watched her run toward him, but that disappeared within her smile as she closed.

"Look what I have," Grace said. She held a piece of paper in her hand and held it out for Barnes to take. Instead, he pulled her toward him and lifted her to sit on his lap. Then he looked at the paper.

Wisps and clusters of crayon reds, greens, and blues colored the heavy paper. "That's wonderful," Barnes said, turning the paper over to see what it looked like with the top side down. "That's nice. Is it a house?"

"No, silly, it's a tree. See." She held the picture at arm's length and studied it herself. "See. It's our yard and trees and the sky and this," she pointed her small finger at an arcing series of reds. "This is the sun."

"A red sun?"

"Mandy had the yellow so I made it red. And you told me about how smoke turns the sun red."

"Yes, sometimes it does. Can I have the picture or are you giving it to your mother?"

"No." She leaned into Barnes and cupped a hand between her mouth and his ear, her breath warm and fluid as she added, "I'm putting it in my secret place."

Barnes whispered back, turning his face to her ear, "Where is your secret place?" She smelled of soft youth and uncluttered innocence.

Grace huffed at Barnes's ignorance and looked at him with a get-real slant to her mouth. She said, "If I told you, it wouldn't be a secret."

"No. I guess it wouldn't." Barnes looked up and nodded to Call, who walked slowly to join Grace and him on the porch. The old man held his unlit pipe in the corner of his mouth, which slanted his smile and creased the skin around one eye. He stopped at the bottom of the stairs to turn and watch what almost became an accident.

A car drove past on Loomis and would have run the stop sign had another car not beat him into the intersection on Mountain, the crossing street. A lean wind stirred the trees and the sun fell lightly on Grace's golden hair.

"It's in the basement," Grace whispered.

"Your secret place?"

"Yes. It's like a little room but it doesn't have any lights so I take my flashlight down there with me. I don't think anybody else knows about it because the door is so small, but I can get in. I think ghosts used to live there."

"Ghosts? Do you believe in ghosts?"

Grace did not immediately answer Barnes's question. She turned her picture over in her hands as she talked. She said softly, "Ghosts of other kids. I haven't seen them but I know they're there. I go down there with Harp and play sometimes."

Call climbed the steps and stood facing Barnes. He sighed loudly. Grace slid from Barnes's lap, her conspiracy broken, and hugged Call's leg. He placed a hand on her shoulder to return her hug.

"Oh, darling," Call said as he hugged Grace's head against his jeans. "You had best never run away because these old legs will never catch you."

Call sat in a wicker chair across from Barnes, and Grace sat on the porch's top step. "How you doing this day?" Call asked Barnes.

"Just enjoying it."

"There's plenty about the day to enjoy." Call pulled from a coat pocket his roll of pipe tobacco. With a dexterity that belied his age, he scooped the tobacco into the pipe's bowl and tamped it down with the closed end of his pocket knife. He lit the tobacco with a wooden match ignited on the seam of his jeans, and pulled softly at the pipe to blow a subtle plume of smoke into his lap.

"You look like you're enjoying the day's end yourself," Barnes said, inhaling the slight drift of pipe tobacco. It reminded him of whiskey and leather and weathered wood.

"I am. I had me a fine day. Ruth is moping about the house, but me and Gracey-girl are doing fine."

Grace raised her head from the picture she had laid on the wooden floor. Her smile passed from Call to Barnes and both men smiled back, captured for a moment as the sun landed softly along the little girl's head and shoulders.

"I'm going to get Harp," she said and stood.

"Don't go inside the house," Call said to her as she skipped down the steps.

"Why?" she stopped and asked.

"Because I asked you not to," Call said.

"Why?" she asked again.

"Because . . . Gracey-girl," Call leaned to sit closer to Grace, who stood on the stair's bottom step, "just think about it."

Grace did. She blinked and looked at her feet and turned and walked slowly. "Okay," she said, then skipped into a run.

"And bring Harp right back here. Don't go off on another of your walks." She was nearly out of earshot as Call finished his instructions.

They both watched her dash off, the wind dancing her hair in the soft afternoon light. She was something to smile at, a girl so innocent that her motions and movements were tender and principal.

Barnes did not think that, but he felt it as he smiled at Grace's skipping shadow.

"I finally found an answer to the 'Why' question," Call said to Barnes.

"I'll try and remember that."

The two men sat in the sun and the company of each other without speaking. They stared at cobwebs on the ceiling and watched another car pass on the road. Barnes let himself drift in the warmth. In the tender sun of that afternoon, their neighborhood seemed like a calm and controlled place, and Barnes bathed in that comfort.

Barnes asked, "Why is it your day was so good?"

"I beat The Rover three straight games."

"Don't you usually beat him?"

"That's beside the point."

"And that's it?"

"I've had some mighty fine company this day. . . . And if you don't quit your fishing, that's going to end right quick."

Barnes laughed and leaned back in his chair.

"If she's not back in a couple of minutes, one of us is going to have to hunt her down," Call said, turning to Barnes with the age lines around the corners of his eyes and mouth doing a light dance with his smile.

Barnes nodded without opening his eyes, "I'll go."

"Good man," Call said.

Barnes rubbed his eyes open. After all the rain that had drenched Fort Collins that spring, the sunshine seemed unusually bright.

"I thought you might," Call added and smiled, settling into his chair. The smile eventually faded from his face. He turned his head and spoke toward the street, not looking at Barnes and not really speaking to Barnes, "That son of a bitch Robert wouldn't walk across the street to find her, his own daughter. I should have kicked his lousy butt the first night I met him. I felt like it then and I should have."

Barnes let the dust settle around Call's anger. He said, "Without him, you wouldn't have Grace." Barnes did not understand why he felt compelled to support Robert even so halfheartedly. He did not like the man any more than Call did and, like Call, thought Robert was Ruth's one big mistake.

"Thanks for reminding me," Call said with satiric scorn. He puffed feverishly on his pipe to bring it back alive and then brushed a honeybee from his sleeve. He took a moment to look through the smoke from his pipe, then said, "The thing about it is that his daughter is only five and she's already twice the person he'll ever be. He's worth piss. I swear . . . either Ruth cheated on the bastard or he passed on some mutated gene to get a girl as good as her. Grace ain't his, I swear."

Barnes felt for the moment like he was standing on the rim of a volcano. He took a moment to step away from the fire. He shifted in his seat and leaned forward with his elbows on his knees. He asked, "How is Ruth?"

"Ta bueno," Call said. He tipped his old Stetson back on the crown of his head and his eyes traced the sunlight waver from a rushing cloud. He added, "She's a fighter. She'll be okay. She'll . . ." Call let his words fall. "She's doing her best. It'll take some time before she realizes that she's moved on, before she can live with her past enough that she can start to see her future again."

"If there's anything I can do . . ."

Call laughed, "Where the hell were you a dozen years ago when she needed you?"

"Probably kicking around in the smoke of some fire."

Neither said anything. The line had been crossed. It was unmarked, no line in the sand, no chalk line on the cement. But both men knew vaguely that they had crossed some line. The sun's warmth turned hard as sheet metal. They had woken into the realization that the past was impossible to forget, that it could and would return in the innocence of a passing comment. And Barnes fully realized in that moment that the pull of the past could reach him at any time.

"I had best check on Grace," Barnes said. He stood and walked past Call toward the steps leading down to the sidewalk. He patted Call on the shoulder as he passed. The movement joined them for a moment, like a handshake joins two men, but neither man looked at the other out of a passing embarrassment.

Before Barnes could retrieve her, however, Grace was running, followed by Harp, a black Lab with a face as good as the early morning. Barnes stood on the top step and watched as Grace and Harp played a quick game of tag and chase on the grass. Then they settled into a serious game of tug-of-war before each decided to search out something different. Grace found a stick and began punching holes on the lawn, which was still soft from the spring rains. Harp paced between the front yard's two sections. The soft pad of his feet on grass was interrupted by the click of his toenails on concrete when he crossed the sidewalk leading to the front steps.

Barnes returned to his chair and sat back down across from Call.

"You've got to face it," Call said. He looked hard and straight at

Barnes, his eyes flat and narrow but not unkind. "You have to face it," he repeated.

"I know," Barnes said, looking from Call down at the painted wood of the floor. Since last summer, since the fire that killed half his crew, he had felt left behind, a remnant left by life.

"It's not easy," Call said. "It will be the hardest thing you ever do, but you have to face what happened and accept that you did not cause it."

"I just keep asking the same question, though," Barnes said. "I keep asking 'Why?'"

"Barnes," Grace said from the lawn. Her body looked tiny and fragile.

"Yes," Barnes answered.

"Just think about it."

With Ruth in the kitchen and Call upstairs reading stories to Grace, Barnes stood in the familiar theme of Call's office. Although Call held a doctorate, he did not keep his diplomas on his wall. Hung there were photographs of his time—his family and his war. He had returned from Asia with medals and wounds and dreams and nightmares, then returned to teach history at the university in Fort Collins. After retiring from teaching, he continued to read and write studies of the past in hopes of understanding the future. Mostly, though, and in the last handful of years, he listened for his granddaughter's song.

Barnes stood in the arcs of light tossed haphazardly by the room's floor lamps and studied the photographs hung on the office wall. The room was neither lavish nor ostentatious, nor was it naked or impersonal. Like Call, there was no single striking feature in the room, but everything, the oak desk to the photographs to the dark cherry bookcases filled with hardcover editions, was right, and each accented the others in simple dignity. The single set of double-hung windows looked out onto the front porch and from there toward Mountain Avenue, a much quieter street when Call first moved his family into the house.

A wardrobe-sized cabinet held rolls of maps in its cubbyholes, each map detailing elements of some European battle Call had written about. The two leather chairs Barnes and Call often sat in to share Bushmills showed the dimpled impressions of their bodies. A single book waited between a stained pair of leather coasters on an end table. A filled magazine rack sat next to Call's chair.

Barnes studied the photographs, one in particular that cast a small group of soldiers inside a grained haze. Call was one of the soldiers barely distinguishable from the others in their T-shirts and helmets. They huddled together with all of the braggadocio of youth. Barnes knew from past talks that the photograph showed Call on Christmas Eve of 1965 in the jungle near Cu Chi. He looked into the photograph and felt as though he were inside a synthesis of moments, the memory of those moments becoming more real than the present.

He saw his face reflected on the glass fronting that photograph. Inside the frame of his reflection he saw himself standing on a hastily constructed helispot above the Tempest Ridge Fire the previous August fourteenth. Dust and smoke flew and hovered around him like a dry fog. The ground smelled baked and the air's heat was intense to the point that he imagined his walking caused a dry wake in the parched air.

His first thought as he walked to the side of the helispot was that the fuels were far less sparse than they had appeared from the recon flight, that what had looked like a predominantly rocky slope was actually covered with dead and senescent scrub oak as high as twelve feet. He wondered quickly whether the diamond area, the crew's safety zone on the side of the hill, was also different than it had appeared from the helicopter.

He had dialed his radio to crew net and called Chandler. When Chandler answered, Barnes calmed his voice before speaking, "Where are you?"

"Head of the line."

"I'm on H-2, but I can't see you or the crew. Where are you in relation to H-1?"

"From H-1, the line drops down the ridge about a hundred yards, then cuts west across the top of the burn. We're about another hundred and fifty yards along that. It's slow going. The fuels are more dense, more continuous than we thought, a lot more cutting with the saws, but we're making headway."

The wind blowing up the drainage where Barnes's crew worked pushed steady and dry. Barnes could feel the wind drying even more as it warmed and quickened up the canyon's chute. He felt his lips begin to crack from the wind and his sweat dry even before it could begin to roll down the sides of his face.

The air that blew against and across him was only the bottom of a mass of dry, cold air that had poured across Colorado's Western Slope as a fast-running stream follows its fluvial bed. Thousands of feet above the ground, the air flowed smooth and straight without a hint of turmoil. Lower it eddied across the topography of valleys and ridges, swirling in its own turbulence until funneling as a torrent through the gaps along the western edge of Colorado's Rocky Mountains, and eventually, and soon, and without Barnes or anyone else knowing until too late its full ability, the wind would blow like a great bellows to push the fire across and up the slope and over his crew.

"I'm not so certain I like what's happening here."

"Why's that?" Chandler was breathing hard, and the staccatoed breath over his radio did little to ease the tension Barnes felt.

"This front we're getting feels stronger than a little wind change. There isn't a cloud in the sky, so this little front they told us about is one dry mother. The winds are still from the south and are already picking up, so we're getting an increase in the wind speed and the front hasn't even hit us yet. I don't like it," Barnes said, his words as dry as the wind. Barnes understood the possibility for tragedy riding with the wind, but he did not know how completely his world sat uncertainly on the forward edge of that wind. At any moment, the wind could break and his world could tumble.

"We're okay, Barnes."

"Talk with Max. See what he says." Barnes wanted to just order Chandler to start the crew off their line and back to the safety of a helispot but he also did not wish to break Chandler's spirit.

"Max is out front scouting the fire."

"Rest everyone where you are and have them gather their gear. I'll call Max and talk with him."

"Barnes, we're fine. The fire isn't doing anything."

"Just rest the crew until I get back with you." He wanted his voice to form in calm determination, but the clenching tone of anticipation snagged his words.

Barnes turned his radio to fire net and called Max Downey. Eddies of dust pirouetted around the ridgeline where Barnes stood and he knew with certainty that the cold front predicted for that afternoon was something greater than he had been told. Barnes could see a column of grey smoke building in the canyon's bottom but its origin was covered by the ground's roll and a series of small spur ridges.

Barnes spoke rapidly after Max answered, "I don't like this, Max."

Max laughed, "Don't get soft on me, Barnes."

"This is no joke, Max. Things can go south real quick. I think you should hike it back to the ridgetop on the double."

There was a dry pause before Downey answered. "We are close to tying off this line," he said. "I'm out ahead of your crew and I'm not worried."

"I can't see the fire from H-2 but I can see a small column building below you."

"I see it also. It's within the fire's perimeter."

"The winds are getting bad up here and if your fuels are anything like up here, you could be heading into trouble."

"Listen, I talked this over with your squadie, Chandler, and he and I agreed that we can dick this mother."

"Max, if this wind keeps picking up, all hell's breaking loose. Your line won't hold even if you can tie it off."

"It's my fire, Barnes."

"It's my crew and I want them heading out now."

"You want this fire, Barnes? Damnit, do you think you can run this fire better than me? You want this fire?"

"Yes. Now. Double it back up the line to H-1. We'll finish our pissing match there."

"It's still my fire," Max said. "We can tie it off and line out and catch any spots. But if you or your crew can't handle it, then I'll call in some Type-II crew that will."

"Max, damnit, listen to me—"

"You worry too much, Barnes. You're like a mother hen cluck-ing over her chicks. We've scouted the line and with you and a couple of jumpers as lookouts, we'll have plenty of time to get out if we need to."

Barnes flinched when Ruth touched his shoulder. She left her hand there. After a moment under the warmth of her touch his muscles loosened. Sweat that had formed on his hands and neck cooled.

"Dad refers to this as his rogues' gallery," Ruth said, stepping next to Barnes and slipping an arm inside his to hold him close. "One day when my mother was still alive, Dad said he was going to take all of the photographs down and cover the wall with another bookcase. She told him 'No.' That was all, just 'No.' And he didn't. She said that her disagreement had nothing to do with the books that needed a place other than in boxes. What she did not want to see happen was Dad lose his footing, her words, lose his footing by forgetting the man he was."

Barnes leaned toward the photographs. "Your mother was a smart woman."

"Yes, she was," Ruth agreed.

"I wish I could have known her."

"I wish I would have known her longer."

Barnes straightened one of the photographs that had rested off-level, forcing the half-dozen men to look as though they were being emptied into the side of the frame. From upstairs there came a de-lighted peal of a little girl's laughter.

Ruth giggled. "He does that sometimes," she said.

"What?" Barnes followed Ruth's eyes in looking toward the stairs and the light shrouding the landing in softness.

"He sometimes tickles Grace just enough to wake her up so he can read another story to her before she falls asleep. I've told him that she needs her sleep more than another story or she won't be able to stay awake during the day. He just puffs on his empty pipe and smiles."

"He's earned his little chicanery." He looked back at the wall of photographs. "I bet he was a fun son of a bitch to know back when he was young, like here." He pointed toward the photograph.

Again Ruth scanned the photographs on the wall. "That one," she said, pointing at the grainy image Barnes had been studying when she joined him in the room. "That one is my favorite, always was. I used to look at it and wonder what he was thinking. In the corner, if you look, you can see 'Christmas 1965, Cu Chi.' I still come in here every Christmas to look at it. He once told me how scared he was then, how scared he was every minute he was at war, but especially how scared he was then, over Christmas. I would sometimes come in here and look at him there because I never believed my daddy could be that frightened."

"We're all scared sometime."

"I suppose we are. I guess we just don't realize how scared everyone else is."

Barnes nodded and glanced across the room. A wall of filled bookcases stared back at him. The corners of the books had whispered frays from being read, and gold book darts marked significant passages. The room between where he stood with Ruth and the opposite wall of books was large, but there was no feel of emptiness nor of randomness. Here was a view of the man who used the room.

"You care for a cup of tea or are you drinking whiskey with the old man?" Ruth smiled as she spoke. She often referred to Call as the old man and sometimes mimed his habit of naming a shot of whiskey a "snort."

"No, not tonight," Barnes answered. "Tea sounds good, though."

She walked past him and he followed. Fragrance from Ruth's perfume drifted lightly behind her. Barnes inhaled it, holding it for a second longer than necessary. As he passed the stairway, Barnes could hear the muffled voice of Call reading a story to Grace. He concentrated for the slight moment before he moved beyond the man's words, but he could not make out what story was being read. Just the melody of Call's voice, however, was enough for Barnes to smile. He could see that voice hover softly and wrap around the closing eyes of Grace, kissing her eyelids closed and enveloping her in a warm embrace of sound.

The suddenness of the kitchen's light was bright and intrusive. Barnes blinked as he entered the room. He stopped just inside the doorway and rested his back against the door's frame. He watched Ruth take a cup from the cupboard and thought how beautiful she was. He could see a danger in her, a wildness harnessed but a necessary wildness nonetheless. In the angle of her smile and the light of her eyes he saw the hints of what was not tamed. She had never acted the role of a temptress, never invited him in that way, yet she formed his temptation. Even when he had almost fallen in love with Maria Lopez, he had still felt the vague and distant tug of Ruth. And since the death of Lopez on Tempest Ridge, Barnes had wakened at nights from dreams of one woman to thoughts of the other. His legs would search out remnant cool spots between his sheets and his head would roll onto the fresh unweathered folds of his pillow, and he could feel and smell the women who were not there.

They had never admitted it nor spoken of it, but Barnes knew they had both acknowledged a longing in their glances. Watching her then, as she stretched to take hold of the cup, he wondered at what point does the wrong thing to do suddenly become the right thing to do.

"I already made a cup for me. The water's still hot." Ruth turned and said, "What do you want?"

"Earl Grey." He crossed his arms and looked down at his feet. He felt himself blush like a kid in junior high just caught dropping his pencil so he could bend down to see what he might see.

Ruth reached into another cupboard to take a box of tea bags. "Milk and sugar or honey?" she asked.

"Raw sugar."

"I like that." She poured his tea water and scooped a spoonful of sugar into it before offering it to Barnes.

"You like it that I asked for raw sugar?"

"No, no, not that. That you didn't say, 'Whatever,' or something like that. I hate it when I offer something to someone and they say, 'Whatever.' Like they think they're doing you a favor by not being specific. That saying, 'I don't care,' is anything less than acknowledging their non-interest."

"Well, you asked, I answered."

"I know. It's that simple, but some people. That was one of the first things that made Daddy mad at Robert. He came over for a barbecue and Dad asked him what he drank. Robert said whatever he was having was fine. Polite, but noncommittal. I asked him how he wanted his salad, and Robert said, 'Whatever.'

Finally Dad asked how he liked his burgers, and, of course, Robert said, 'However.' So Dad burned the burger black as new charcoal."

"I can see that." Barnes held the cup of tea close to his face to let the steam frame his mouth and cheeks.

"To deciding," Ruth said, holding her cup at arm's length toward Barnes. He lifted his and nodded his head.

Ruth drank from her cup, then said, "I haven't seen you leave for work this week."

"No," Barnes said. "I decided to take the week off. Hunter can handle anything that comes up at the office, and I need some time to get prepared."

"But you are going back?"

Barnes, without looking at Ruth, knew she was studying him. The scenes in his mind played out in mixed fashion. Although not as certain about his words as he was about how he wanted them to sound, he said, "Yes. I just needed a break before the season begins, before things start rolling."

He met Ruth's smile. Hers was the smile of understanding and knowledge. They looked at each other for a long moment before Ruth turned toward the refrigerator. She took out a plate of cinnamon rolls and set it on the counter next to her teacup. The rolls were inviting, topped with a glaze of icing.

"I didn't have dinner today so I thought I might have a late snack," Ruth said, taking a plate from the cupboard. "You hungry? Care for a roll?"

"I'm not hungry, but I'd still like one." He put his cup of tea on the counter. There was always a roll or sandwich or bowl of soup, along with drinks. Since he could not reciprocate in turn, not with his bachelor's refrigerator, he at one time had wished that Ruth and Call would not so often go to the trouble. The evening he had mentioned that to Ruth, Call answered quickly, "God-damnit, Barnes, if I didn't want you eating my victuals, I'd boot your butt out." It was not a matter of receiving, Barnes realized, but of giving, and although he did not always accept the offer, he had come to welcome the attachment.

Ruth placed two of the rolls on small plates to warm in the microwave. She and Barnes dropped into a steady silence within the oven's hum.

"How are you doing?" Barnes asked.

"Without Robert, you mean?"

Barnes nodded, "Or with Robert."

"No, it is most definitely without Robert. . . . Not hot and cold anymore, maybe just warm and cool. Which is good, I guess. And which shows you how far along to separating we were in the first place. That road is not one we just lately took the entrance ramp onto. We've passed the speed limit already and have just been on cruise control for a good while."

She handed him the plate with his roll on it. Whiffs of steam wavered above the roll. Barnes looked at Ruth's hand as she withdrew it, slim and long and tan.

"Warm and cool, I guess," she repeated. "Tepid maybe."

"Tepid is good then?"

"I suppose. It's a numbness, like the center of a storm before you can start again. It's that necessary stage you go through when being numb is preferable to feeling. It's nice for a while and hopefully it's short-lived, and finally you come out the other side and all at once you start to feel again. I'm looking forward to that, to feeling some of the pain again so that I know I'm not yet dead. And since I got a jump-start on the numbness, maybe it will end soon."

Ruth sighed and blinked. She shook her head as though thinking over what she had said.

Barnes looked out the kitchen window. A cat's-eye moon was supposed to rise, but a light mist had already captured the night. The mist turned into a drizzle and Barnes wondered if the coming fire season would be a washout.

Barnes watched Ruth as she ate. Her hair swung long against her back in slow-motion waves of deliberate brown. The brown of her eyes glinted half-tamed and strong and sharp, and her lips, slightly over-large as though bruised from kissing, curved slowly in a full red arc. Everything about her held a small shock of surprise that drew Barnes toward her. But it was not her beauty alone that drew him. It was that her body hummed. He wanted hard to step into her melody and be danced by it.

"Maybe," Ruth said, then she paused for her last bite of cinnamon roll. "Maybe, I'll take a drive this summer, in a couple of weeks after school ends. I'll take a scenic route somewhere, not like driving with Robert. Hands hard on the wheel, you know, like driving is serious business. No, I'll just drive a while and stop. Maybe go down by La Veta, where I spent a few summers back in my wild woman days."

"See how many cafés have been replaced by Kentucky Fried Chickens?"

"Don't say that."

"Or how many coffee shops say Starbucks?"

"Barnes, you're going to wear out your welcome real fast if you keep popping my bubbles."

"Just kidding. It sounds like a good idea. Would you take Grace with you?"

"Maybe. I don't know. I might leave her here with Daddy. They do well with each other, sometimes I think better than she does with me. Certainly better than she does with Robert." She lowered her head for a moment as she placed the two plates in the sink. "Robert wanted a boy. It wasn't some macho thing, you know, like some women think men are like. It wasn't that he wanted a boy he could teach about cars or something like that. He didn't want a girl because he's afraid. He won't admit it, but I remember the look on his face when he saw Grace that first time . . . in the delivery room and the doctor handed her to him. He was scared of her, not that she was this little thing, this little baby, but that she was a girl and he just didn't know what he would do. How do you raise a girl? I could see the question across his forehead light up like a neon sign. I knew then that I would, someday, be raising her alone."

"Not all alone."

"No. I'm glad you're around as much as you are."

"I didn't mean me."

"No, I know. I just wanted to say that, to say that I'm thankful you're here. But, yes, Dad. I wish I would have appreciated him more when I was younger."

"That wasn't your job. Kids are supposed to hate their parents. It's a rule or something, like not understanding their mortality. I fought with my parents, you fought with Call, and someday Grace will drive you crazy. It's all written down somewhere."

"Yes, but that's not exactly what I mean. I don't mean the battles. I mean appreciating or respecting what he provided. Little things I was too stupid or blind to see. I remember when I was a kid on

Sunday mornings. Dad would get up early, before Mom or me, and come downstairs and cook breakfast. He would set the table, squeeze the juice, and make pancakes, flapjacks he called them, or these incredibly decadent omelets with three cheeses and fresh veggies and deli ham. Oh, God, it was heaven when Mom and I would wake to that smell wafting into our bedrooms. Heaven. First that smell and then softly the sounds of Dad working at the meal and Mozart, always Mozart on Sunday mornings. I would roll out of bed and toss on my robe and run down the stairs. We would sit, my mom and I, and Dad would first serve us and then sit with us. I'd say thanks, sometimes, but I didn't really fathom what it all meant, why he did it. You know?"

Barnes nodded. His own parents had been good people who had gone too early. One day he was ignoring them and the next he no longer had the opportunity to tell them what they meant to him. Standing in the sudden light of Ruth's kitchen, he felt a vague hollow at that recognition of not just who he had lost but also what that loss intimated.

Ruth said with a smile, "I just don't understand why I didn't want to marry a man just like the man who married dear old Mom."

"Another part of growing up, I guess," Barnes sighed.

"You're full of mournful wisdom tonight."

"He's full of something but it's not wisdom." Call limped into the room and clasped Barnes by the shoulder. "What are you two doing down here while I'm up comforting the little girl?"

"Comforting, my rear," Ruth said. "I heard you wake her so that you could read another story to her. I know you. Don't give me any of your Irish blarney, old man. I've lived too long under your roof to be fooled by you."

He shrugged slightly against Barnes, letting his body fold into itself. He said with an adopted brogue, "Oh, but it's a sad world when your own daughter speaks to you in such a way. An old man like myself."

"Don't come looking to me for support," Barnes said.

"Another dagger. I had better brace myself with a spot of the poteen. Care for a snort, Barnes?"

"Thanks, but not tonight."

"Oh, but the civilizing influence of women." He shook his head with a show of dispirited woe until a smile lined his face. He used Barnes as a support to raise himself straight again, then stepped to the counter.

Ruth said, "You are just too full of it, Dad."

Call winked at Ruth and retrieved a bottle of whiskey from his cupboard. The rest of the kitchen cupboards held a communal array of foods and spices and utensils, but Call's cupboard was his alone. At the end of the line of glassed doors, he kept his cupboard stocked with bottles and old-fashioned glasses together with wooden and tin boxes of treasures for himself and his friends, one holding a stash of dog bones for Harp.

He poured a couple of fingers' worth of Bushmills into a glass and turned to face Barnes. Holding his whiskey between them, he toasted, "May the wings of liberty never lose a feather."

Barnes nodded and met Call's toast with his teacup, feeling, suddenly, a touch inadequate.

"What were you two doing down here?" Call asked, sucking on his lips after the first taste of whiskey.

"Just talking," Ruth said.

"About?"

"Why? Were your ears burning?" she answered.

"Ruth was saying what an SOB you were when she was growing up."

"Barnes."

"Guilty," Call said. "Sometimes you can hug too tight."

"Actually, she found me in your study looking at the photographs on your wall," Barnes said.

"The ancient and the not-always-honorable, my past in rust." He toasted again before drinking.

"You sound as though you're especially invigorated tonight," Ruth said.

"Just full of vinegar is all. That wonderful girl of mine upstairs told me I was the bestest grandpa in the whole world. It just struck me as being a particularly wonderful thing for her to have said. Charges the circuits."

"We were just talking about that."

"What?"

"Those nice little compliments," Ruth said as she brushed past Call. "I'll go tuck her in again." She turned and gave Call a kiss on his cheek. "Thanks, Dad, you're the bestest."

She walked from the kitchen into the shadowed hall. Barnes listened for her sound to recede up the stairs, the wood groaning and creaking in response to her steps.

"I don't know exactly what has happened, but I like it," Call said.

"Just talk," Barnes said.

Harp nudged Barnes's leg, offering his lazy muzzle for Barnes to rub. Then the dog tested the wood floor and padded over to Call. He looked up expectantly, his legs spread wide for support and his tail wagging.

"He doesn't quite trust the floor," said Barnes.

"No. He can't really see it too well. Probably thinks it's one big hole, the way he gingers himself across it. He likes big rugs and his fat dog bed on the floor."

"You better hope nobody breaks in through the kitchen or he may just not attack."

"He never was worth much in that way and now he's just worthless. Aren't you, old boy? You are a worthless hound," Call said, scratching the dog's ear. He reached back into his cupboard, taking a couple of dog bones from an old cookie tin his father had liberated in Germany to send to Call's mother. "You can't see, can't hear, can't bark hard enough to scare a dust mite. If you weren't as old as me, I'd put you out in the street."

Call handed a bone to Harp and Harp broke the bone into pieces, chewing one end and dropping the rest onto the floor.

"You had best lick that floor clean, hound, or you and me will both be out on the street."

Harp sniffed and ate the remaining crumbs left on the floor. He nudged Call's leg.

"Worthless. You hear me?" Call leaned toward the dog, holding another bone close to his muzzle.

Harp growled.

"What?" Encouraging the dog.

Harp barked, a soft backward bark like an old man's cough.

"What?" Holding the vowel out a little longer to further encourage Harp's response.

A louder bark.

Call placed the bone on Harp's muzzle and signaled the dog to stay. Harp sat motionless, eyes elevated and pleading up at

Call. Call said, "Okay." Harp flipped the bone in the air and tried catching it in his mouth. The bone, however, bounced from the tip of his nose onto the floor, where he merely picked it up and ate it.

"Worthless," Call said, running a hand down the dog's back, then walking from the kitchen.

Barnes followed Call. They walked back into the warmth of Call's office. Call sat at his chair, then Barnes sat. It was a comfortable routine, a sovereign groove that promised a momentary stability. Call filled and fired his pipe. "Which photograph were you and Ruth looking at?"

"The one in Cu Chi. Christmas, I think."

"Christmas, 1965. It was hot, Jesus Christ, hotter than a poker, but, anymore, I can't really recall how hot it was, just that it was hot. And how much I didn't want to be there. You had to keep in the shade, which wasn't an easy thing to do on a hilltop firebase scraped perfectly clean. The only shade was in the jungle below us, and that was over-filled with Charlie. We went out on patrol just after that photo was taken and that kid next to me, Voznesensky, the little one who looks even more frightened than the rest of us, never came back. He'd joined us just a week or so before, fresh from home and bam, he's in the middle of it all. Voznesensky, I didn't even know his name then, was killed inside a tunnel the day after Christmas. We found the tunnel outside a little Vietnamese village. I called it in and was told to check it out. Voznesensky was a little guy and cherry-new, two qualities that didn't bode well for him. When I looked into the black hole of that tunnel opening, all the vets knew what was coming. One of them said to send in the FNG. It didn't matter, though. I had already tapped Voznesensky for the job. He stripped off his gear and dropped down inside, a .45 in one hand and a flashlight in the other. After a few minutes, we heard some fighting—a .45 and a bunch of AK-47. The AK-47 ended it. Voznesensky was dead. No two damn ways about it. I waited another fifteen minutes with everybody else in the squad staying in their perimeter posts and avoiding my eyes, just in case I decided to send down another mole. I sat there and watched that hole and listened, but nothing. Oh man, some holes that we stare into are too dark and deep and black. There's a part of me that's still looking down that hole, hoping that kid comes wiggling back out and the last thirty-seven years have been nothing."

Call paused and smiled an embarrassed smile, then continued. "I was convinced if I sent someone else down to pull out Voznesensky, that he'd die as well. We tossed in a few grenades, left, and called in Air to pummel that hill, burn everything on it and turn the rock to sand. But I left Voznesensky down there. As he was stripping his gear, his fingers couldn't undo his belt they were shaking so badly. I helped him. I told him to buck up, to take it easy and slow, and if he found anything to scoot back out and tell me. I told him that the VC knew we were coming and had probably already left the tunnel for the next province. I told him that at least he'd be down in the shade and out of the sun. He smiled. I gave him the thumbs-up. Never saw him again. I can still see his eyes. They, he, trusted what I told him, that he'd be fine."

For a long time neither man spoke. Each relived his own raw moment in time when the world and all the people in it suddenly stopped, when the fragile endings of life unraveled in exact violence. It was a moment Call had known for a long time and which Barnes was realizing would stand still forever, stretching unbounded ahead of them, a moment of such infinite suddenty for which a certain price had been paid in the loss of a man's soul.

"I couldn't stop it," Barnes breathed.

"And I couldn't stop what happened, either."

Barnes felt a weight on his chest. "But I could have, if I'd been there first and seen it."

"And I could have too, maybe, had I known what was going to happen."

"How long did it take for you to get past it?"

"Haven't yet."

Barnes rubbed his eyes.

"Some men are lucky," Call said.

"How so?"

"Some men are defined simply by what they do. Some of us, you and me and many others, are defined by how we live with what we have done. It's a matter of how you deal with that day that matters now."

Barnes swallowed hard. He looked away for a moment and silently nodded his head.

Call spoke slowly, his words tinged with years, "You can't believe me yet but you will, I hope. It will take you years to understand what it took me years to understand. What happened in that tunnel and what happened on that fire are no longer what's important. They happened. We can't, neither of us, we can't change the physical parameters of our lives. So what happened to us is not as important as what happens within us."

Barnes thought of himself standing on that ridgeline like a shaman reading blood omens, finding in the whispers of a wind some intimations of his fate. He heard Hunter's last words to

Chandler before Chandler took half the crew to the fire. "Vaya con Dios, amigo," Hunter had said, and Chandler gave them a quick nod, then took long, steady strides to the head of the crew's line. "Mount up," Chandler called. By the time Barnes reached the fire, the world had already begun to turn. Soon the smoke preempted the sun, tinting the world a sepia. Then the fire moved like spilled mercury. And by then, there was nothing he could do but echo lost prayers.

Near midnight, Barnes woke to his bedroom's darkness as though he had not been asleep at all. He walked down the short hall to his other bedroom, his study, the room from which his ghosts always launched. Passing the mirror he saw he was naked and went back to his room for his robe. Back in the study he walked to the desk and turned on the lamp. He pulled two envelopes of photographs from his desk and dumped them into separate piles. He knew each photograph without looking. Each remained fixed in his mind as though it lay in its chemical bath. But he studied each one, hoping that by looking at them he might erase them, lose them from his memory and from his life.

He breathed through his nose, which brought a sharp, burning pain deep into his sinuses. Holding a photograph of Lopez, or a photograph of the charred body of who Lopez once was, Barnes felt a wind gust and saw cattails of clouds blow along the belly of the sky. Sweat rolled down the sides of his face to gather beneath his chin. The fire's noise roiled as loud as a train, and then louder, like a train wreck. A noise which built and circled and formed itself in space, a naked volume racing ahead of itself to swirl around him like demons. The moving bulk of flame and smoke drained the valley, all its air and existence, leaving an emptiness filled only by its own smoke.

Within that riled moment of memory, Barnes realized that he needed to go to the cemetery, to where Lopez was buried, to see her place, although he had visited her grave four times since the fire. Maybe this time he would find the words to whisper to her.

He dressed quickly and left his house without turning on any lights. From the recessed shadows of his dark windows he could feel the eyes of his apparitions upon his back. They did not follow him, but they waited for his return.

Large American elms planted a century ago bordered the cemetery on the west and east; the north was boundaried by Laporte Avenue and the south abutted a golf course. Barnes approached through the golf course. The concordant rhythm of water sprinklers and a smell of fresh-cut grass surrounded him in cool pleasure. Barnes knew the way, even in the dark, and jumped the short fence behind the seventh hole and into the cemetery. He stood for a moment listening to his own breathing and the distant sounds of a small city not quite asleep. He watched the choreography of shadows cast from the moon and trees, filters of clouded light weaving through the elms with their leaves full and heavy.

He walked across the grass until he came to the dirt and cinder road and followed it west until he found the large monument that marked her row. The old stone monument had been engraved in 1912 with a now-fading inscription: "Little Lamb of God, Bless Thee." The monument marked another grave a mother had provided for her daughter who had died too soon. He stepped close, within arm's reach, and stood for a moment to read the inscription, then walked into Maria Lopez's row.

Barnes felt a certain, sudden unease, a tiptoeing fear as he walked through the cemetery. It was not a fear brought on by ghosts, for he lived with ghosts. It was one of judgment.

He found where Lopez lay—a small rectangle of polished gray marble surrounded by wet grass and a single empty metal vase. Barnes stood away from the grave and watched it. He could not distinguish the marker's inscription which he knew read "FATIMA MARIA LOPEZ" and beneath that "OUR BLESSED DAUGH-TER" and the last line "Born 9-1-72 / Died 8-14-02."

The moon threw zigzag shadows across her grass, the relative newness of which cast a dark green boundary for her reliquary. His legs felt uncertain. He heard the engine of a car and the crunch of its tires on the cemetery road. The car stopped a hundred feet from him, the lights dimmed. He could see inside the car the silhouetted figures of two people join together and disappear, a slight rocking of the car, and then silence.

He bent and wiped a hand across the marble. His fingers traced the cold lettering. He knelt at her grave, one knee on the ground as though attached, and his fingers swept across the stone in slow, extended arcs. He knelt for a long time, long enough for another wildness to rock the car and then another silence and fi-nally the car's leaving. He said nothing although he wanted to. He felt his lips not moving, but he wanted to move them as in prayer.

He thought quickly and without intending to of Lopez taking the place of White. White, whom Hunter had caught with whiskey in his water bottles. Needing to send another pulaski for Chan-dler's line, Barnes sent Lopez. White remained in the staging area, Barnes flew to the upper helispot, Lopez walked into her death. He kept himself from damning White but still could think of nothing to say to Lopez.

He had walked down the hill past the stunted bodies of Warner and Doobie and Sully and Horndyke. The fifth body from the ridgeline was smaller than the others, lying alone and away from everyone else and huddled like a flower that had closed into itself with the end of day. Even before he saw the silver inlay on her knife, he knew it was Lopez. Her body, almost too small for a firefighter and then made even smaller as death parched and wizened her body, curling it into itself. Her head lay uphill with her hands and arms tucked in tight. Her fire shelter lay four feet up the hill from her body. It was partially opened as though she had fallen to the ground and then tried to cover herself with it and then the wind had blown the fire shelter from her hands, leaving her with nothing. Of her clothing, only her shirt collar and leather belt remained. Not even her boots were left. Her entire body had charred. She lay alone, nobody else near her. She lay face down, her head uphill but tucked in as though she had tried folding herself around herself. Her daypack lay six feet downhill, so Barnes thought she must have taken a few steps before falling. Maybe, he thought, as dust and ashes filtered about her body, maybe she had recognized a better place to deploy the shelter but just did not get it open in time. When the gust of wind hit her, knocking her to the ground just before the flames would arrive, she must have realized what was about to happen, she must have seen her death in those seconds and prayed or lost her mind or cried out. And left alone with nothing else in her suddenly primal world she pulled into herself.

Standing above her, Barnes felt an immoral imposition upon her.

All he could think to do was place his fingers to his lips and then down on the marble slab. Then he left the way he had come.

He could see her pick up her line gear to join Chandler on the helicopter, not looking back at Barnes as they flew to the fire. He could see her walking into the cache with Budd. He could see her asleep and naked in his bed.

She was dead. He knew that. He had seen her ruined body. He had placed a kissed finger to her mouth.

Chapter Four

THURSDAY

arnes woke an hour before sunrise. He began reviewing the previous August as though he could bid time to return, as though
he held it within the sub-light of a computer screen and could
revise it all. He could only lie there and watch again as the world
skipped a beat. The moon's light, like prevenient ghosts, bent
through his open bedroom window. Softly falling shadows separated
and joined on his walls. His morning had become another roil of
moment and memory.

Even after nearly a year, the memory remained hard and pungent,
circling counterclockwise in his mind.

They had arrived in Craig sometime near midnight and bedded
down at the high school football field. At four-thirty, Barnes woke
with Hunter and Chandler and met with the BLM officials planning
the complex of small fires in the Craig District. By five, the sun was
still only a possibility on the horizon and Barnes knew his crew's
assignment.

Barnes had already bested the five-hundred-hour mark for the
season's overtime and was dog-tired. A chronic bronchitis had taken
root in his lungs. His neck felt like one long ache, and the fingers of

his right hand took longer to unravel each morning. Altogether, a season to dream about. One to take to the bank in a big cart, but also one with a price tag attached. In the last week of eighteen-hour days on a stubborn blaze near Fort Collins that had burned a good part of the university's mountain forestry camp, Barnes had felt his body unwind like the mainspring of an old Seth Thomas and he knew his mind was following suit.

He had been waiting for a fire on which he could allow one of his two squadies to supervise, maybe let Chandler take the crew—Chandler needed the experience and Barnes wanted to spend a couple of days with his head in the dirt. Barnes enjoyed having a crew, having a group of nineteen charges, but sometimes he wished he could just lose himself inside the group of twenty and dig line or cut trees or mop up like a poge rookie. Days and nights spent doing nothing but the immediate always recharged his body and mind.

This fire, still unnamed, barely forty acres and leisurely grazing at the piñon-juniper, sage, and Gamble oak of a southwestern aspect, would become Chandler's—still uncontrolled but not burning with any great intensity, a plan of attack already developed from the previous day yet still in the initial attack stage, a load of jumpers on the hill since the previous morning led by a man Barnes had known for several years.

Walking back from the trailer being used for the command post, Barnes asked Chandler, "You listen to everything they told us?"

"No," Chandler said. A moment later he added, "Hell, Barnes, of course I listened. It's only the beginning of August."

"It's the middle of August," Hunter said.

"Hell. I don't need to watch the calendar until November. Until then there are only two types of days—days off and days on and the forest circus tells me which day it is." Chandler raked a finger behind his lower gum to rid his morning jolt of Copenhagen.

They stopped for a moment and Barnes asked, "You want the crew on this fire?"

"Yes."

"Good." Barnes appreciated attitude, he liked when his squadies wanted more responsibility than he had afforded them. He knew that Chandler had wanted the crew since finishing the classroom courses necessary for Crew Boss but had waited through Chandler's insistence for a fire that he felt certain the man could handle. He said to Chandler, "Like the IC said, Max Downey will fly down with the first helicopter flight and then him and us will go up for a recon look while the crew's gearing up."

"Sounds good."

"Max is a good man, a bit headstrong, but still a good man. Don't let him bull you, though. He only knows one way, and that's his way."

"Don't worry."

"He'll start ordering your sawyers around like they're his and—"

"Damnit, Barnes, I can handle it. Don't worry so much."

"I'm not." Barnes turned to Hunter. "Tell Monterey that we'll take all four saws—"

Chandler interrupted him, "Wait a minute, boss."

"What?" Barnes asked.

"Remember who's the top dog today," Chandler said.

Barnes smiled, "It's your show. Take it."

"All four saws," Chandler repeated, "and extra water for everyone—the weather report says hot and dry. Double lunches in our line gear and have Aggie get a couple extra cases of MREs from supply to stage on the helispot in case we coyote tonight."

"Four," added Barnes.

"Four," said Chandler. "Also the same number of cubitainers of water. Get the crew lined out for the helicopter shuttles, but backwards—my squad goes first with me to H-1 and you and Barnes with your squad fly last to H-2."

Barnes again interrupted. "We'll already be on the hill. You and me with Max."

Chandler thought for a moment. "Have Warner line out my squad. You take your squad on the last flight."

Hunter nodded. He checked the list he had written in his pocket notepad.

They walked in silence back to where the crew slept. Seventeen bodies cocooned inside paper sleeping bags, a sonorous melody of necessary sleep rose with the morning. Barnes smiled, then said in a tone slightly lifted from conversation, "Good morning, little darlings."

A few people stirred. Ira stuck his head out from the opening in his bag like a turtle and squinted toward Aggie, who sat in her bag next to him.

Aggie said, "Go away. You're just a bad dream."

"I've got your bad dream right here, Aggie," Warner said from the other side of her.

She turned. "What you got is nothing more than a fleeting thought."

"All right. Listen up," Chandler said. "Right now let's get breakfast, gear up, and hit the line. We'll have a picnic lunch on the hill."

"Who died and made you king?" asked Aggie.

"I'm king for a day, king for a fire. This puppy's mine."

Aggie looked to Barnes. He nodded. She said to Chandler, "You just better not make me carry any damn piss pump. We got rookies for that shit."

"Where we're going there won't be enough water to fill a dew bead much less a bladder bag," Chandler answered.

"Every day's a holiday, eh Hunter?" Kapell said.

"And every meal's a picnic," answered Hunter.

"Hit it hard and keep it small," Doobie added sarcastically.

"Every time I hit it hard, it just gets larger," George answered.

"Shut up," Freeze said as she slipped on her boots. Like the rest of the crew, she had slept in her pants, T-shirt, and socks to allow for every extra moment of sleep possible, but still she woke in a bad mood. She shook her head and looked at George, "Can't you ever say anything that isn't about your damn penis?"

"He's a man," said Aggie. "That's the only thing he knows. First thing in the morning for most of these guys means draining the blood from the primary appendage back to their brains."

"Kind of like jump-starting a cold engine," added Lopez with a laugh.

"A hand crank on an old car," said Aggie. The three women laughed.

"What in the hell did I say?" asked George.

"Too much," answered Barnes as he nudged White's sleeping bag. "Wake up, sunshine. You joining us today?"

"Barnes, if I thought I had a choice, I might just exercise it."

Chandler answered, "Whitey, you're a hot shot. You gave up your freedom to choose in May."

Monterey sang out in a raspy voice, "Saint Peter, don't you call me, 'cause I can't go. I owe my soul to my FMO."

Barnes and Hunter stood away from the crew's awakening to watch the cadence of seventeen people waking from five hours of sleep on a hard ground. Chandler strolled through the men and women, stopping to nudge anyone still asleep. He pulled a snoose can from his back pocket, tapped the lid with the tips of his first two fingers, opened it, and deposited a two-finger pinch between lip and gum. He stood above White as White pulled a long drink from his canteen.

"Sips," Chandler said and reached out for White's canteen.

"You better not," White said, "I got a cold."

"Man, you always got a cold."

"Yeah, maybe I should just stay here in bed and die."

"If you wanted to die in bed you shouldn't have become a hot shot."

The crew slowly gathered around Chandler. They knuckled their eyes, they stood hunched with hands in pockets, they leaned unconsciously against each other. They put off waking as long as possible. Many of those who would not live to see the day's sunset were reluctant to open their eyes to greet their last sunrise.

Chandler repeated the information presented at the morning briefing, telling them of the fire's specifics, the present and expected fire behavior, the topography, the weather. Hunter then read from his list of what additional gear the crew needed.

"A cold front?" Freeze asked Aggie as the crew lined out. "Does that mean it's going to get real cold?"

"You really are a rookie, aren't you?" answered Aggie.

"What?"

Aggie placed her hand on Freeze's shoulder, "While we're eating breakfast, I'll tell you what you should remember from your S-190 class. After that you can come with me and pack water. Whitey and Kapell, you guys come too."

Like a farm truck warming to the day's work, the crew's movement quickened. People rubbed the sleep from their eyes or stretched their bodies or bent and spit parts of their lungs into the grass of the football field or sat as in trances with one boot on and the other held loosely between fingers that did not yet want to work. Before Chandler and Barnes left for their recon flight, the crew had all dressed and lined out behind Hunter. They walked in line to the mess area for breakfast, and Chandler and Barnes walked side by side to the heliport.

Chandler and Barnes waited near the edge of the heliport for Max Downey to arrive from the fireline. They each held a cup of coffee they had picked up in the helitack tent. Barnes had both his hands wrapped around the Styrofoam cup, warming arthritic kinks from his joints. He held it close to his mouth and blew softly across the coffee, forcing a warming steam to swirl and rise to his lips before he drank. The coffee tasted terrible, too weak.

He remembered the fire-coffee he enjoyed when he was on the Chena Hot Shots in Alaska—a couple handfuls of coffee tossed into a stripped-out coffee pot filled with boiling water, let the coffee boil for a couple of minutes, then splash some cold water on top to sink most of the grounds and drink. That may not have been the cognac of coffee, but at least it was hardy and hot. The coffee he picked up from the helitack tent was soft and lightweight. But he drank it anyway, allowing its warmth to heat him.

He stepped to his side to catch the sun's opening rays. In that movement from the night's last attachment to meet the coming day, he knew the day would be as hot as the briefing had promised. He tilted back his head and closed his eyes and drank in the radiant heat. He let the sun thaw him. His body, as it had done on late-summer fires for the past fifteen years, began to respond slowly to the warming. He stretched and felt the kinks and knots from long days on the line and short nights on the ground begin their fight against loosening.

He heard the helicopter approaching from a long way off, sounding like a small grouse thumping its breast. The sound of a Bell 206 Jet Ranger. He turned his back to the heliport to protect himself from the helicopter's rotor wash which spread in dusty waves around him and across the landing field, blowing papers and leaves and hardhats across the field to be captured against tents or trucks or bushes.

Before he turned back around to look at the helicopter, he let it rotor down. Max Downey stepped from the right side of the helicopter, said something back in to the pilot who nodded his head in affirmation, then more out of habit than necessity stooped down to avoid the rotors turning above his head, and walked to meet Barnes and Chandler.

"Say, Barnes," Max said as he reached out his hand.

"Max." Barnes took Max's outstretched hand. They shook as old friends do.

"You don't look so good," Max said, placing his hand on Barnes's shoulder. The men turned and walked back toward the helitack tent and away from the noise of helicopters arriving and departing.

"That's still a helluva lot better than you look."

"And that's a helluva lot better than the last time I saw you. Alaska, wasn't it?"

"Yes." Max had been the division boss on a fire near the Gateway to the Arctic Wilderness Area, and Barnes had taken a squad from his crew to catch a finger of the fire as it burned up and over a ridge, threatening to ignite a stand of dog-haired black spruce and taking off on a run that would not have stopped until it reached the glaciers. Max had set the plan in action and told Barnes what he wanted. Barnes took his ten people and went head-on with the fire along that ridge for six hours before they finally contained that section. It had twice jumped his line and they scrambled to knock it back. Once the fire made such a rush through the black spruce that he had to call his people to a hastily constructed safety zone to wait out the run.

Standing on the perimeter of the heliport, that fire in Alaska seemed to Barnes further back than the six years that had passed.

Barnes introduced Chandler to Max, and the three men leaned against a truck to talk. Max carried a growth of beard a few days old. The sides of his face were stained from dirt and from where the sweat had run rivulets through the dirt to expose a sun-reddened skin. His hands were cracked and dirty and scarred, and he coughed when he spoke.

Max said, "It was too dark for me to fly down for the morning briefing, so I didn't hear what all was said. You guys can fill me in on all that. I'll tell you about the fire before we jump on the ship and take a look-see at what we got up there." He pointed over his shoulder at the hill where their fire burned.

Barnes followed Max's fingertip and looked at the fire burning indolently, looking more lethargic than threatening. He could see no flames but a soft, light-gray swirl of smoke. The fire looked from the base of the mountain as though it was already kicked. He liked that. He wanted the fire for Chandler to work out and for himself to regain some of what he felt he had lost over the course of the season.

Barnes and Max leaned against the truck's quarter panel. Chandler stepped away from the truck to face them. Max propped his foot on the running board like a cowboy hefting his boot on the bottom rail. Chandler explained the basics from the briefing. Since the camp was working on a complex of fires, nothing had been said specifically about their fire, mostly general information about the weather followed by even more general discussions on topography and safety and the desire of the incident commander to have all fires contained by ten o'clock the next morning. The fire they were assigned to had been named the Tempest Ridge Fire, a forty-acre blaze within the much larger Craig Complex of eight fires burning in the area.

Chandler handed Max a copy of the day's briefing report. He read out loud while Max and Barnes read along: "Light winds out of the southwest at fifteen to twenty-five, shifting to northwest and increasing to thirty with passing cold front about fifteen-hundred. Diminishing cloud cover in the morning, skies will be clear in the afternoon. Chance of rain: ten percent. High temps: 87-95. Low Rh: ten to twelve percent."

"Looks like a hot one. Did they call it a red flag?" Max asked.

"No," Chandler answered. He looked to Barnes, who nodded in agreement.

Barnes added, "They didn't say anything specific about fuels either, just that most of the fires in the complex are burning in piñon-juniper and brush and Gamble oak."

"Yes," Max said. "That's what we got, too. A lot of that oak. What did you say? Gambles oak?"

"Gamble oak."

"When we're in the air, we'll take a look at it but you won't see much. It's just barely burning up there, not much really. We got a line down one side and across the ridgetop to connect the two helispots. I think we can dick this puppy in a day or two. If they aren't giving us a red flag warning, then they must not be too concerned with that passing cold front this afternoon. Just a light wind with reduced temps."

They talked a little more about the fire season, a general banter to loosen themselves to each other. They compared overtime hours and where they had been and when the last time was that they had slept in a real bed or drank a slow beer. They talked of how they might spend the winter.

Barnes asked Max about his family.

"My daughter, Joanie, she turns seven in a couple of days." He looked at his watch. "Two days from today. We'll be off this smoke-job by then but I won't be home. Hopefully I'll be back to Junction by then so's I can call her."

Barnes nodded in agreement.

"You married yet, Barnes?"

"No."

Chandler added before Barnes could continue, "He's married to his job."

"God, a lifer."

"Aren't we all?"

They walked together to the heliport. Max told a helitack person that they were ready to board their helicopter for a recon flight. The Jet Ranger lifted slowly from the grass field, hovered a moment before dipping into its turn, and rose quickly above the ground to circle the fire.

Max rode in the right front seat next to the pilot, with Barnes and Chandler in the rear. They all wore headsets with microphones and talked within the helicopter's metronomic whop. From the air, the fire appeared even lazier than from the camp as it grazed around the ridgeside, consuming little and with what it did consume taking its time. Barnes surveyed the forty acres within the fire's perimeter looking for signals, looking for the bells that should sound an alarm.

They flew in slack circles, talking mostly in crisp, short sentences about the fireline, the fuels, the topography, the expected weather, and what Max and the other jumpers had seen the previous day and night. Max told Barnes and Chandler that very little had happened on the fire. A few fire brands had risen into fire devils, circling and dancing like small, burning dust twisters. "No big thing," Max said. "A couple of quick runs up the west side with flame lengths of fifty feet or more, but that was all well within the perimeter. Nothing spectacular."

"Not much," Max continued. "You can see our line down that west flank from the helispot toward that diamond-shaped area."

"What's in that diamond?" Barnes asked.

"Mostly rock. It'll serve as our safety zone."

Max paused then added with a smile, "Ain't no-thing."

"If you tie into that diamond, you may have it," Barnes said.

"We got it dicked." Max answered, nodding agreement.

"Looks steep," said Chandler.

"It is. Near the top of the ridge it gets to about fifty percent, so we have to be careful of rolling rocks going down that line and while we're mopping up."

"And that's where you want us? Along that west flank?" asked Chandler.

"Chandler, you'll come down with me along that line. We'll strengthen it and then just below the diamond, we'll come across on the south side there. Your squadie Barnes," he paused a moment to let everyone smile, then continued, "they'll improve the line across the ridgetop between the helispots, from two to one and burn out the top. By tonight we should have a good line around three sides of this puppy and finish her off during the night."

They finished one flight through the canyon and turned to begin another.

Barnes asked, "Can we get a little lower? I'd like to take a look at that diamond area."

The helicopter dropped a little and slowed some so that they could study the ridge.

"It doesn't look all that safe," Barnes said.

"It's good," Max said. "We can cut it back a little if you want. But we should be well past that spot and hooking the south side before that cold front hits us. And when we get down there, we'll have the burn and all those grassy areas for safety zones."

They returned to the base heliport. After leaving the Jet Ranger, they stood again near the trucks they had first talked by. Chandler walked off to find Hunter and brief the crew while Max and Barnes waited near the helitack tent. Barnes marked on his map the locations of helispots and the diamond area and drew lines where the firelines would be and marked the general boundaries of the fire.

"That is steep," Barnes exhaled as he studied the contour lines of his map.

"Yes, it is," Max answered.

"And that diamond area didn't look all that secure."

"What's the point, Barnes?"

"I'm not so sure about that line on the west side."

Max exhaled loudly. "I was on that line all yesterday afternoon and it's good. We haven't quite got down to that diamond area, but—"

"Wait a minute. You haven't been there yet?"

"No, we—"

"Wait. Have you scouted it?"

"We are now. I have a man scouting the line now."

"So you don't know how good a safety zone it is?"

"It's good, Barnes. That fuel looks just like alder. Jesus Christ. Listen, if your crew can dig any line at all, we'll have this fire lined quick as shit."

"Look at where the hell your line is."

"I was there. I know the line."

"You're digging downhill with a fire burning below you and your best safety zone you don't even know if it's a safety zone at all."

"It's good, Barnes. If it isn't, we'll have a meeting on the hill and decide a new plan."

"I don't know."

"What? What in hell don't you know? I'm the IC on this fire, Barnes, but if you want to pull your crew out, all right. That's your choice. Do it now, but don't start pussying on me."

"Just listen, Max."

Max kicked the ground. "Man, I don't need this shit. I'll find a crew that'll do what I ask. Take yours back to camp and babysit them."

"Problem?" Chandler asked. He and Hunter stood a couple of feet away from Max and Barnes. A swirl of dust tossed up from a departing helicopter briefly encircled them and they squinted to see through the haze.

The rest of the crew sat or stood another twenty yards back watching the two men. Barnes did not realize until then how close he and Max stood, that the toes of their White's boots almost touched.

"Barnes wants to sit out this fire," Max said.

"What?"

Barnes explained to Chandler his misgivings about the fire plan. Max stood with his arms crossed, looking at his boots and shaking his head. He walked a couple of strides away, turned, and walked back. His jawline tightened as Barnes talked.

Chandler looked from man to man, gauging not just his desire but also his loyalty.

"I had a good look from the helicopter. I think it's okay," Chandler said. "You gave me the fire. I'm making the decision that I'd make if I were alone."

Barnes rubbed his eyes. He felt trapped and tired. "Listen to me," he said. He looked first at Max and then at Chandler. "The fuel type is Gamble oak, not alder, and it can burn hot and fast and can sustain runs without having a ground fire to support it, so the possibility of reburn is high with this fuel. Second, the slope is steep, too steep maybe and you're building the line downhill toward an active fire."

"But you saw it," Chandler interrupted. "It's hardly burning at all."

"Right," Max agreed.

Barnes held up his hand. "That's right now. But look at the weather. It's been hot and dry for weeks. The fuel, just look around here, the live fuel is bone dry and will dry even more as the day passes." For emphasis, he picked up a small pine stick and snapped it between his fingers. "And then you have a cold front coming in this afternoon."

"But no red flag," said Chandler.

"Right. If there were much danger from that front, they would have issued a red flag warning," Max said.

"You'll still have the wind change."

"Hell, you always got wind changes." Max turned away again and took two steps before returning to where Barnes stood. He faced Barnes square. "Just tell me what in hell you're going to do. If you don't want up there, then stay here. If you don't want your crew up there, then walk them back to their sleeping bags. I'll find a crew that will do the job. We aren't pushing the envelope that hard here, Barnes."

Chandler said, "You gave me the crew for this fire, Barnes. You shouldn't have done that if you don't trust me to make the right decision."

Barnes looked down at the ground. The grass near his feet had begun to die from a lack of moisture and the presence of people walking across it all day long.

"I'm not taking this back from you," he said to Chandler. "I . . . It's your crew and your call."

Barnes did not see Chandler's smile nor the smile that flattened across Max's face. He looked at Hunter, who nodded in agreement to him. He did not, however, feel good about his decision to let Chandler make the call. He did not know whether he would have kept the crew from this plan of attack or if he was just playing the mother hen or if he was just tired.

Chandler said, "Good. We'll be going in three loads. The first load from my squad will go up with Max and me. The second load, with the rest of my people and Horndyke, Hassler, and Warner from Hunter's squad, will follow us." He pointed at Barnes and Hunter, "You two can take the last trip up with the rest of Hunter's squad and secure the line across the ridgetop. Barnes, you should find a place along the ridge for lookout. If anything changes, you tell us and we'll book out of there."

"The ridge should make a good lookout," Max added.

"Okay," Barnes said. He squinted into the emerging sun, watching it rise into its warmth.

"You don't have to play this conservative for my sake," Chandler said.

"I'm not," Barnes said.

Max nodded and walked away with Chandler toward a waiting helicopter, a Bell 212 large enough to carry Max and the Red Feather crew's first load of firefighters, their tools, and extra food and water. The helicopter would ferry the two squads to the fire in three trips, then wait in support to shuttle more equipment or firefighters if needed or to sling a load of bladder bags filled with water or to hook on its two-hundred-gallon water bucket for water drops.

White stood at the end of Chandler's squad as they waited, collars up and shirt sleeves rolled down, to board the helicopter. Barnes and Hunter stood a few feet away.

"You worried?" Hunter asked.

Barnes nodded.

"About Chandler? He's a good man."

"No, not about Chandler."

"That jumper then?"

"No. A bit. Max tends to overestimate himself and underestimate the fire."

"You think that's what he's doing here?"

"I don't know. I'm probably overreacting. He's a damn good firefighter, but sometimes he thinks he can bull a fire."

"I wouldn't worry much. We'll be up there soon and can take a good look from the ridge. If it's not good, we'll just back off and figure out something that's better." Hunter checked his watch, then shaded his eyes to look at the fire. "It's only six in the A.M. That puppy ain't even woken up yet. Either we'll kick the shit out of it before noon or we'll find a better plan."

"I know. I don't want Chandler thinking that I don't trust him."

"He'll do fine."

"We going to be here a few minutes?" White asked.

"Why?" Hunter answered.

White, who had placed his gear at the end of the crew's line, looked up from where he sat. "No reason. Just deciding whether I should open a book or not."

"No. You'll be on your way as soon as that 212 powers up and helitack calls us over. Fifteen-twenty minutes tops."

White retrieved a water bottle from his waist belt, stood, and opened the bottle for a drink.

Warner, standing in front of White, leaned his head against Freeze's shoulder. "Just wake me when it's all over," he said.

Freeze elbowed Warner in the stomach, knocking him into White and causing White to drop his open water bottle. The water drained and spread into the dry sand, staining it the color of wet cement.

White bent to retrieve the bottle and kicked dirt across the spilled water.

The scent of whiskey brushed past Barnes and Hunter.

"Let me have a drink," Hunter said. He took a few quick steps toward White.

"Sorry, Hunter, I got a cold."

"I don't care if you got AIDS. Let me have a drink."

White looked from Hunter to Barnes. His face drained of color as he handed the plastic bottle to Hunter.

Hunter sniffed it and touched it to his lips. "Let me taste your other bottles," he said as he handed the bottle to Barnes, who took it and smelled.

"Damnit," Barnes said.

"What now?" asked Max from the front of the line.

"Nothing that concerns you, Max. Chandler, you better get back here."

Chandler walked back and watched Hunter open and smell from the second, third, and fourth water bottles. He handed each to Chandler, who in turn handed the bottles to Barnes. None of them said anything. They did not look at each other nor down the line of men and women waiting to board the helicopter.

Barnes turned. "Come with me, Whitey. . . . And bring your line gear." He walked away from the crew followed by Hunter and Chandler. White picked up his line gear, slipping his arms inside the shoulder straps of his pack but leaving his waist belt uncoupled and dangling at his hips.

Twenty feet from the crew, they stopped.

"You stupid bastard," Barnes said. His face flushed, and he could feel his eyes harden. His entire body tensing, he drew in a rigid breath to calm himself before speaking. "I know this shows a problem we have to deal with, but right now all I can think of is how damn stupid you are."

"Barnes, I—"

"Shut up." His voice sounded high and thin, almost a whine. He clenched his fists and exhaled all the stale air from his lungs in order to regain himself.

White continued, "It's not what you think. I don't need this. I can take it or leave it."

"The leaving it I'm not concerned with. It's the taking that's got me upset." His voice felt more in control even though he felt that the morning was gradually slipping from his grasp.

"I'll just fill new water bottles."

"No. I'm not taking any chances with an alcoholic on the line. Stay in camp and we'll deal with this when we come off shift."

"I'm not an alcoholic."

"Stay in camp," he repeated, this time more slowly as though he were speaking another language.

White stood facing Barnes. He said nothing and stared into Barnes's impassive face, catching the flashing glints of anger crossing through Barnes's eyes. His shoulders drooped from the weight of his line gear. He walked off toward the waking commotion of the fire camp.

Barnes moved slowly past Hunter and Chandler. He paused a few steps away to catch his breath and loosen some of the tension in his muscles. He turned and walked back to stand with them. For a moment they all remained silent. Finally Barnes spoke to Chandler, "You better take another digger with you."

Chandler and Hunter turned to look at the crew. Chandler ran a finger under his gum and tossed the spent Copenhagen onto the ground. He retrieved his can from the back pocket and scooped another pinch. Whenever he had the time to think, he took a moment to replace his Copenhagen. It was a habit he had assimilated from Barnes a few years earlier. And even though Barnes had since quit dipping, Chandler still used the exercise as a praxis.

Chandler thought out loud, "I'd be inclined to take Aggie, but she's the best pulaski you have and you may need her if the digging gets hard along the ridgeline. Monterey and Ira got saws and George is a good shovel man. If I take Kapell, that leaves you with Aggie and Lopez as your pulaskis, and I wouldn't curse you with two women. So I'll take Lopez with me. She'll ride in the first load." He spat again and turned to Hunter. "Sound good?"

"Sounds good."

"Good. Let's get this road on the show."

Chandler hit Hunter in the middle of his chest with a heavy tap and walked off to tell Lopez and to join Max Downey at the front of the line. Barnes noted how a change had become apparent in Chandler over the morning, how in the few hours since they woke Chandler had grown more accustomed to giving orders. His voice had developed authority and he approached the crewmembers with less familiarity. Barnes thought that was good, that Chandler had adopted his new position and was taking it seriously.

White had disappeared into the staging area and Barnes turned his attention back to his crew. He felt a constriction in his throat and an ache in his left ear, and he knew that a cold was working its way into his body.

He sat with a groan on the running board of a truck. He looked down the line of firefighters readying to board the helicopter and noted that none looked as tired as he felt. They were all young, some over twenty years younger than Barnes, and most were in better shape. What they had as a result of their youth that

Barnes could feel slipping from his body was a resilience, an ability to bounce back more easily from days and nights of humping across ridges or slumped over to dig a line or mop up a stump hole. And even though they averaged only five or six hours of sleep a night, they had usually fallen asleep well before Barnes slid into his sleeping bag and woke an hour following him. He envied them their youth and wished he could be twenty again and just beginning his fire career.

"Mount up," Chandler said.

"Vaya con Dios, amigo," Hunter said.

Chandler waved.

The first load followed Chandler to the helicopter, 39D in large red stencil along the boom. Its rotors spun with a lazy surety as they stepped in, one following another. A helitack person carried the racks of tools and placed them under the back seat and then put the two chainsaws and Dolmars of fuel and oil in the boom compartment. Barnes could see Lopez and Budd sitting in the hellhole on the helicopter's near side.

With that first load of Red Feather Hot Shots aboard, the helicopter's rotors swung faster, and the helicopter slowly lifted, then hovered and dipped and swung and flew off for the ridge.

A whirlwind of dust tossed by the helicopter's rotor wash swirled around Barnes. He dropped his head to his chest, pulled tight the collar of his shirt, and clenched his eyes against the dust storm. When he looked up, the helicopter had already begun its long climb to the ridge.

Barnes looked at those who waited for the second load. For a moment he studied Warner. The sleeves of Warner's Nomex shirt were rolled down, collar up and top button fastened, as they were supposed to be. Barnes had fought long and hard with Warner about basic safety, that he would be more likely to survive the fire following a crash if he had his Nomex covering him as much as possible. At first, Warner just replied that he'd probably die in the crash anyway; eventually, though, Warner followed practice.

As the helicopter disappeared behind the ridge, Warner pulled the strap for his hardhat down below his chin. His safety glasses were already on. A glove was on his right hand and in the fingers of his ungloved left hand he rolled an ear plug. His line gear lay in a heap at his feet.

Barnes thought of how Warner liked to carry an extra water bottle instead of his fire shelter in the shelter's case strapped on his belt. He called out to Warner, asking where his fire shelter was.

Warner laughed and answered, "For Christ-sake, Barnes, I already got a mother—it's where it's supposed to be."

Barnes started to reply, to ask to see the shelter in its case on Warner's belt and not in Warner's backpack. He even raised his arm toward Warner, but felt deflated by the notion of another small conflict. He sat back and thought, "Go ahead and burn up, you stupid bastard."

The helicopter returned to pick up the second load and again disappeared over the ridge. On its return for the last load, however, the Bell 212 veered south before approaching the landing pads and flew off to the southwest toward Grand Junction.

A helitack woman walked over to Hunter and Barnes. She was dwarfed by her flight suit and helmet. Both men leaned down to hear her over the whine of other helicopters approaching and leaving the pads.

"Thirty-nine D flew to Junction for a while," she said.

"Why?" Hunter asked. Like Barnes, his hands were on his hips as he leaned in toward her. A quick gust of rotor wash swirled dust around them and they all closed or covered their eyes as the dust dissipated.

The helitack woman said, "To pick up somebody important who wants a look at the fires."

"Couldn't they finish our shuttle first?"

She shrugged. "You guys are only fighting the fire. What makes you think that's more important than some asshole from Washington, DC?"

"What crap."

"Tell me about it."

"Can we finish our shuttle with another ship?"

"We'll do that as soon as we get the other crews to their fires."

"How long?"

"I don't know. We're running low on pilot and helicopter hours, so we'll see how everything shakes out. Your fire is low-low on the priority list."

"Not to me."

"Yes, but you're not in charge of this cluster-fuck." She shrugged again and walked off to the helitack tent.

"What's the word?" Aggie asked when Barnes and Hunter joined her and the rest of the squad.

"Hurry and wait," Hunter said.

"Same old song," she said, as she sat and pulled a paperback from her daypack. She turned so that the morning sun came over her shoulder onto the book.

Monterey and Ira pulled the bars of their chainsaws onto their crossed legs and began sharpening the chains. George walked to the helitack tent to see if he could scrounge or steal a Pepsi and recent newspaper. "Heli-slugs always got some good shit lying around. I'll just find me some." Kapell lay on the ground next to Aggie with his head on his pack, pulled his hardhat over his eyes, put ear plugs in, and slept in the dust of the field. Hunter walked to the Port-a-Johns. Barnes looked up at the ridge and shook his head. He felt a tightening in his throat and stomach. He drank from his water bottle to wet his lips. For the first time in years he wished that he still chewed.

Aggie put down her book and said, "Don't be such a mother hen, Barnes."

Barnes smiled and nodded.

Soon after two in the afternoon, Barnes and Hunter and the others boarded 39D to fly to the ridge. The morning had been a six-thousand-foot August morning with a cloudless sky, high and clear as a diamond, with thin air and the promise of an afternoon of oppressive heat. The fire that had been burning slowly, just grazing at the brush and grass, began to stretch and toss fingers of flame restlessly into the sky as if to catch the air. As the helicopter passed the fire's flank on its approach to the helispot on the ridge, Barnes watched a long flowering of flame spiral to the left.

When 39D landed, Barnes led his crewmembers from the helicopter. He did not turn to watch the helicopter lift off from the ridge to return to fire camp as the others did. He walked to the edge of the hastily constructed helispot and looked down on the fire beginning to churn below him.

The sky was then high and violent, and the wind was already changing. Barnes could feel the wind against his face. He heard it rush across the leaves and dirt of the ridgeline like a felon memory, a strong and hungry, dry-toothed wind. He suddenly felt removed from himself, watching himself as in a photograph on that ridge looking down into that canyon. He had landed in a raw place in the heat of summer.

Sunrise, his house had not yet filled with daylight heat but Barnes lay drenched in sweat. He turned on his radio to listen to the news, a continued savagery in Africa, a continued unrest in the Middle East, a continued famine in Asia. Images of men and women caught in a snarl of pain flashed through the opaque borders of his consciousness. The weatherman promised a change, a sunny day with little chance of rain followed by a quickly passing dry cold front and increasing winds. He blinked and clutched his fists, holding against a swirling wind. At Coors Field the night before, the Rockies had split a close doubleheader with the Giants, winning 16 to 9 and losing 21 to 18. Like debris in a current, harrowed faces rushed across his mind.

His eyes closed. His ghosts came from down the hall. They walked past his doorway. Each took a moment to look in on him. He saw them without opening his eyes and imagined them walking down the slope, walking like blind men walking. A tightening in his throat gripped him and he shook himself alert, his breathing tentative, his fingers shaking.

The room was calm, no breeze even through the open window. Everything was motionless and silent as fear in a wide wilderness. The only sound he thought he heard was that of dry twigs and senescent grasses crunching under heavy boots.

He lay in bed until the telephone rang at almost seven-thirty, and then he stayed there until Ruth's voice came over the answering machine, "Barnes? Answer, Barnes. We have a mission."

Barnes pulled himself from his bed to pick up the telephone. "Mission?" he asked. "What kind of mission?"

"My dad said he has another date this morning. I've got to find out what the hell he's up to."

"Don't you think that if he wanted you to know, he'd tell you?" He rotated his neck to rid some of the kinks and saw himself in the mirror looking like Lazarus on the last day.

Ruth said, "Don't be so damn puritanical. Of course it's snooping. I know that, but after all, I'm his daughter. I have a right."

"You do?"

"Yes, I do. You sound like you were born in the Northeast."

"All right, let's not get personal."

"So, you with me?"

"Do I have a choice?"

"Of course you do. But I'll never cook any more cinnamon rolls if you don't come with me."

"This may take more than cinnamon rolls."

"I don't have time to barter. He's downstairs getting Grace ready for school. As soon as he's driven off, we'll hop in your truck and follow him."

"My truck's a little conspicuous for this sort of thing."

"Okay, my car. But you drive."

"Do I have time to shower?"

"No. Just get dressed and keep watch out your window."

She hung up without saying good-bye.

He dressed in Levi's, Chuck Taylor's, and a Fat Tire T-shirt, made himself a strong cup of coffee, and stood watching out the front room window for Call and Grace to walk to their car. When they did, Barnes hurriedly brushed his teeth and was out the door before they had rounded the street corner.

Ruth had already backed her Volvo from the garage. She got out to let Barnes behind the wheel and then skipped around to sit in the passenger seat.

"We know he'll take her to school first, so we can wait down the street from that."

They drove down Mountain Avenue a couple of blocks behind Call and Grace.

Ruth was dressed similar to Barnes in jeans and T-shirt. In her lap she held a pair of binoculars and a newspaper.

"You're serious about this, aren't you?"

"Damn right, I am."

"No guilt?"

"No."

"What's the burr that's got you so worked up?"

"He's had dates with women before and never been as secretive as this. Something's up."

"Like?"

"Like I don't know. That's why we're doing this."

They followed Call to the elementary school, waited for him to leave off Grace, then followed him again back downtown where he parked and walked to a coffee shop. They parked across the street from Call and watched him through the Volvo's front windshield. He entered the coffee shop, sat at a window table, and opened his newspaper.

"Convenient of him to sit there," Ruth said, peering through her binoculars at the window.

"Maybe too convenient," Barnes said with a poor Russian accent.

She put down the glasses and frowned, "Who are you—Boris Bad-accent?"

"Who?"

"Never mind. Just pay attention."

After a few minutes, a man joined Call at his table. They shook hands, talked for a moment, then the man placed a small box on the table.

"The Rover," Ruth said.

During their talks on the porch, Call had told Barnes about The Rover. His real name was Billy Rinaldi and he had been in the war with Call. In Vietnam he had been wounded when a mine had exploded near him, and since then he wore a metal plate in his skull. He was eighteen when Call sent him as point on a patrol to meet the end of his youth. Rinaldi had had a dog named Rover when he was young, and after returning from the war with a section of his brain replaced by metal, he answered only to the dog's name. The Rover had his own house, but spent the length of each day walking through Fort Collins, beginning most days with a cup of coffee and a game of dominoes with Call.

A young girl sat at another window table. Until her mother joined her, Barnes wondered if the girl had skipped school. The girl took off her hat, and Barnes could see the patchwork of her hair, as though she were molting. The girl ignored the stares of others, and Barnes wondered at her strength. Why a girl so young had to suffer that, and how a girl so young drew such courage.

Nearly an hour later, The Rover left and Call sat with himself, his coffee, and his newspaper. He worked leisurely at the coffee and newspaper, alternating his attention between the two, enjoying each, it seemed to Barnes, as though they were intended as separate courses of a meal. Barnes drew his own comfort in watching Call with his morning ritual. Call's ease warmed him. At the same time, however, the thought of intrusion pinched at him.

"This isn't right," Barnes said abruptly as Ruth held the binoculars to her eyes. He interrupted a silence of more than fifteen minutes that had lasted since The Rover had exited the café.

"Oh, Barnes," Ruth said as though beginning a much longer sentence, but it ended there with her breath.

"I'm going over to ask him," Barnes said.

"Ask him?"

"Yes, ask him." He reached for the door lever and Ruth put her hand on his shoulder.

"What?" he asked.

"Tell me something."

"What?"

"Why are men the way they are?"

"What?"

"You're repeating yourself."

"Just the word is all."

"What?"

"Nothing. What was it you wanted to know?"

She scratched at a loose hair that had fallen across her brow, putting it back in place behind her ear. Barnes followed her fingers. He felt young and lonely, and he reached a finger over to help her fix her hair.

She smiled and asked again, "Why are men the way they are?"

"Because of women, I suppose."

"No. Why can't you guys just tell us about yourselves, tell us when something is happening inside of you. You make everything such a guessing game."

Barnes sat back in the seat, resting himself against the leather upholstery. He smiled, "I guess, I don't know, because maybe we are more comfortable with ourselves, more comfortable trying to work things through before passing them on to others."

"Comfort?" Ruth asked and shook her head. Strands of hair again slid down along her cheek.

"It's like the therapist they wanted me to see after the fire last year. I went once but all she did was ask questions. I have plenty of my own, more important and more difficult than the ones she was asking. I mean, what I wanted were answers, not more questions. It doesn't make sense."

"And so you think women are like, or want to be like, therapists and place men on a couch?"

"Something like that. Or maybe put us underneath a microscope to see how we tick."

"What makes you think that's what we want?"

"I don't know. You tell me, you're the one asking all the questions."

"Oh, shut up."

"Just trying to help."

"What do you know?"

"We're simple animals, baby, not that complex. Nuts and bolts, duct tape and baling wire."

"What do you know?"

"What do I know? After all, I'm just a man."

"Shut up. Look." She pointed through the car's window at the coffee shop where Call had been joined by a woman. Ruth put the binoculars back to her eyes.

A car pulled into the parking space next to theirs. The driver gave Ruth a double take as he left his car, and Barnes suddenly felt very small.

Ruth spoke slowly through her concentration. "She's tall and well-dressed. I've never seen her before but she obviously knows Daddy very well. They're holding hands on top of the table. They're talking serious. She's let go of his hand and is getting something out of her bag. Who is she?"

"You're asking me?" Barnes could see everything that Ruth was telling him but he let her narrate the scene, let her offer a play-by-play analysis.

"She's reading to him. Daddy reached over. He closed whatever, a folder, that she was reading from. She laughed. Who is she?"

Barnes did not answer. He knew that Ruth was now asking her father this question and not him.

"She laughed again. She's beautiful. You think Daddy and her . . ." The question trailed off into air.

They watched Call and the woman for nearly a half-hour as the city began to come alive around them. Other stores opened and the owners pushed wide brooms across the sidewalk to clean off the cigarette butts and sand that had accumulated overnight. A few early shoppers pushed aside the morning on their way to various stores. A couple of businessmen or lawyers, carrying their breakfasts in one hand and briefcases in the other, passed in front of the coffee shop. Barnes recognized one of them as Ginrich, the refined bit of bad news who represented Max Downey's father.

When Call left with the woman, Barnes and Ruth sat in the front seats of the Volvo staring through the windshield at the coffee shop. A soft silence lay across them, which Barnes interrupted. "What do we know?"

"I don't know," Ruth said. She turned to face Barnes. "I never thought I'd see Daddy with another woman. It's good, I guess."

"You'll have to ask him."

Barnes started the car and drove back home. He would go fishing that day, spend the morning casting and walking and having something not very important to not worry about. He felt as though he had been sliding back and forth between different categories of life, as though every day was a sudden spin-the-bottle of experience. The notion of a world composed within the slow arc of a fishing line settled him.

He and Ruth said little after they parked her car. She went inside her house, and Barnes retrieved his rod and reel from the dust of his basement. He drove up the Poudre, stopping above a wide spot in the river less than a mile from the mouth. No cars passed him as he gathered his case of flies and the rod and reel from the gun rack. He leaned back against the truck with the sun in his face as he strung the rod and tied his fly. He left the road and walked down the slope to the river.

A fire had burned the slope not too long before. Maybe a month, Barnes thought, based on the blackened grasses, not much after the end of the snow. He considered the possibilities—probably a windy day, for the heavier fuels would not yet have dried and the grasses dead from the previous year would have carried the flames; a tourist driving the canyon tossed a cigarette butt out his window;

the still-hot end of the cigarette landed in a bunch of high grass; the wind heated it and drove the embers into flame and across and up the grassy slope; it would not have had the strength or length to jump the road for a run up the hillside and was probably dead before any fire trucks arrived.

He slipped and caught himself by his free hand. The raised, quarter-sized scar left from a burning ember showed purple as he pushed himself away from the ground, the blood from slight exertion pushing through his hand. He left a solid handprint in the ash. The palm of his hand had blackened and before wiping it clean on his pantleg, he smelled the lost aroma of this small fire.

The smell triggered his memory as the sound of a generator could trip thoughts of awakening to the morning fire camp, or a helicopter's thump could pull back expectant waits on a helispot, or chainsaws cutting into a tree's wood, or a shovel's handle in his palm. Rapid-fire thoughts of how he had come to be formed.

He looked across the stretch of burned hillside and saw the green tops of shoots of grass pushing through. The green of the new grass struck him as almost too alive. Then he looked into the river swirling against the rocks and then slowing into gentle ripples.

The sun was still in his face and cast shadows back on the scarred slope he descended. He looked down the river's course, followed it until it rounded a corner and disappeared within the glints of light. The river's water was clear and cold around his jeans and Chuck Taylor's, shocking him when he walked into it. He spent the rest of the morning fishing along that strip of the river, releasing the only two fish he caught. That afternoon, with the sky high and open and the sun warm on his back, Barnes returned to the hillside and retraced his steps back up through the blackened scar.

The late-afternoon sun shined full on his back as Barnes leaned under the hood of his truck to screw the idle another quarter turn out. He then started the truck again and listened, smiled, and patted himself on the knee. After turning off the old truck's engine, he again walked to the truck's front and reached to close the hood, whistling. "Just like a kitten."

Ruth asked, "What?"

In the harsh light bouncing from the hood and windshield, Barnes did not at first catch sight of Ruth. He closed the hood but not hard enough for the latch to catch. Without fixing the hood, he shaded his eyes to see her standing on the curb. She wore the same white T-shirt with a cowboy print on it and Levi's she had on that morning, and Barnes could see small drops of perspiration on her forehead and in the hollow below her neck. He answered, "Nothing. Just talking to myself."

"Talking to yourself?"

"Nobody else to talk with."

"And I thought only old men and married people talked to themselves." Ruth, carrying a hemp bag of groceries in one arm and a six-pack of Newcastle in the other, leaned against the rounded quarter panel of the truck. She placed the bag on the curb and the six-pack on the truck's hood. Tracing a finger across the truck's surface, she said, "A little rusty."

"Just surface. A little body work and some new paint and she'll look ready for the prom."

"It ain't the only one needs body work and a new coat of paint."

"You feeling a little sorry for yourself?"

"And don't you think I have a right?" She pulled a bottle from the six-pack and offered it to Barnes. He took it and knocked off the cap on the truck's bumper.

"I think you're better off now than at any time since I've known you," he answered. He tilted the bottle toward Ruth in a toast, "To the wings of liberty."

"May they never lose a feather," she answered while opening a Newcastle for herself, meeting Barnes's toast and drinking.

He drank, then rolled the bottle across his forehead to allow the condensation drops to cool him. He watched her bend her head back to catch the sun's warmth. Her eyes were closed, and he could see her pulse in her throat. Dimpled with perspiration, the slight beat caused her throat to shimmer in the sun.

Ruth opened her eyes. Barnes watched her eyes follow the three-legged squirrel, Tri-pod, across the road. Her glance darted from Tri-pod to an advancing minivan. She began to touch her mouth with a finger as the squirrel stopped in the middle of the minivan's lane. Barnes turned to watch also and leaned instinctively to push Tri-pod along. The squirrel, as though jacklighted on the pavement, stood staring down the car until he jumped and scurried across to the telephone pole.

"I thought he'd become a pancake there," Ruth said.

"He's gutsy. I'll give him that."

Ruth brushed back her hair and bent to pick up her bag of groceries.

"I thought you worked at the library today," Barnes said quickly, not wanting her to leave. He wanted to hold her presence with him for a while longer. For the moment, she formed a thin veil of solace, and he breathed in the words from her as though they were infused.

"I just couldn't convince myself to go in."

"Call in sick?"

"I've used up all my sick days. I called in dead. Told them that when I was resurrected I'd be back."

"And how long will this take?"

"About the time some poet on a Harley stops at this intersection."

"You may have a wait ahead of you."

"Until then, I guess, I'll sit in my attic room by the window, knitting shawls and living my life at a slant."

"Or you could put on red pumps and a go-to-hell dress and go dancing."

"There's a thought for this poor girl." She lifted her bottle to touch against the neck of Barnes's Newcastle.

Call's El Camino rounded the corner to park against the curb. Grace, in a great gasp of joy, opened her door and ran to Ruth, who bent to greet her. For a moment the world collapsed within their hugs and smiles. Barnes leaned against his truck to listen for a few moments to their pleasure.

Through the windshield of his truck, he could see Call grimace getting out of his vehicle. Arthritis had stretched its tendrils through his joints at an early age. Even though the man's joints often worked against him, once his feet touched the ground and he began to walk, he steadied. The eventual tranquility of his gait made it easy to forget the man suffered in his joints as well as from the remnant pain left by his shrapnel wounds. Below the shadow cast from his Stetson, Call's reddish face gleamed like high clay. He smiled at Ruth and Grace in their embrace and nodded in communion to Barnes. While Call's body suffered from his war and his movements often looked to be those of a man older than his seventy years, his smile kept the warmth of youth.

Call patted the side of the truck with his open hand. Even with the sun behind him and his hat shading his eyes, he squinted when he looked from Barnes to Ruth and Grace. He took his unlit pipe from the corner of his mouth and smiled again.

"Good day, Call," Barnes said.

Call pushed back his Stetson. His voice dulcet and soft, he answered, "But today is a fine day. A good day for baseball, huh, Barnes?"

"A good day to play two."

"Hah, yes."

"Didn't you, Grandpa?" Grace asked. She had turned her head inside of Ruth's hugging arms to look at Call.

"Didn't I what, sweetheart?"

"Didn't you promise me I could have a popsicle soon as we got home?"

Call shook his head and looked down at his cowboy boots. He looked back up at Ruth out of the corner of his eye like a kid caught and said slowly, "I guess I did."

"Daddy," Ruth said, her eyes sharp and straight into Call.

"He said so," Grace said. "Grandpa's not a liar."

"This one time, okay. But any more, little girl . . . and old man . . . popsicles wait until after dinner." Ruth let Grace down. The girl turned to run for the house and her treat.

After a step, though, she turned back to face Ruth and said, her voice filled with expectation and sudden sadness, "Is Daddy home?"

"No, baby," Ruth said, bending down and beginning to reach for Grace. "No. Maybe tomorrow."

"Is he gone forever? Is he dead?"

"No, he's not dead. He's just gone for a while. He'll be back."

Grace walked to her house without saying anything else. Barnes could see the questions circling her, questions the little girl was unable to ask much yet try to answer. In the center of those circling questions, bare and harsh in the sun's light, was the same 'Why' that Barnes knew well.

Ruth stood. Her shoulders hunched, her hands trembling. She rubbed the tips of her fingers across her cheeks, then held them to her lips. She watched as Grace rounded the front corner of their house. With a heavy breath, she sighed, "Goddamnit. How do you deal with that?"

She had not asked Barnes or Call and neither man offered her an answer. Barnes could not even think of an answer to offer her.

Without saying anything more and without looking at the two men, she picked up her bag of groceries from the curb and her beer from the truck and walked after Grace. Barnes watched her leave only for an instant before he opened and shut the truck's hood again, this time hard enough for the latch to catch tight. He felt a heaviness in his eyes.

"I hope he doesn't," Call said low.

Barnes looked at him and his look carried the question.

"I hope he doesn't even come back," Call repeated. Call looked straight at Barnes, then at his house and continued, "It would be hard on that little girl, and her mother also, but him leaving would be the best thing that could happen. Robert isn't much of a man . . . not enough of a man, anyhow, to keep himself right. He's got the best things a man can have right here and he's probably off thinking he's got a life. They'd both have a hard time getting over it but if he left, Grace would be better off. If he comes back, you'll have to keep me from shooting the bastard."

Barnes knew Call meant it. People who disturbed Call's world did not fare well. Barnes turned his face, though, at the quick image of Call, naked other than a pith helmet and his Red Ryder BB gun, taking a bead on Robert in the driveway.

"You know, Call, I'm glad you and I are friends," Barnes said.

"You should be," Call said.

"But I've got something to tell you that's going to piss you off big time."

Call said nothing. He wiped his brow and leaned against the truck's quarter panel waiting for Barnes to continue.

"Ruth and I followed you this morning and watched you meet that woman."

Call took some time before he replied. He dropped his head as though scanning the road's blacktop. He kicked leisurely at a small rock before speaking. He said, "I'm dying."

Barnes felt like he had skipped a step on his way down a flight of stairs. The jarring words stopped time and movement, and he had to place a hand on the hood of his truck.

Call looked at Barnes and repeated, "I'm dying. That woman is my attorney."

"Why?" Barnes asked, then caught his question and asked, "What do you mean, You're dying?"

"I mean what I said—I'm dying."

"But of what?"

"That doesn't matter right now. I'll tell you everything when I've come to that point. I won't die tomorrow or in the near future. But it's not too far on down that trail."

"Does Ruth know?"

"No. Not yet. I guess now I should tell her. She probably has me marrying that woman."

"I'm not certain exactly what to say."

"Then don't say too much. And don't mention this to Ruth. I'll tell her in a day or so after I've got things settled in my own mind."

"I can do that."

"I'd appreciate it." Call placed his hand on Barnes's shoulder and left it there a moment longer than was necessary for him to straighten. He rounded behind Barnes and walked to his house with a wave over his shoulder.

Barnes drank from his Newcastle, swallowing hard. The day had been made warmer. The beer did not give any coolness nor quench his thirst.

"Robert is a freelance husband," Ruth said that evening after Grace had finished her dinner and left the dining room. Through dinner the conversation had remained off certain topics, pivoting primarily on Grace's interest in dressing the dog, Harp, like a ballerina and in Barnes and Call's discussion of the night's baseball game on television. Ruth had mostly remained silent, and neither Barnes nor Call wanted to begin something that might end with Robert's name or presence being called up.

When Grace left the room, carrying her empty plate in front of her, however, the room emptied into silence. The walls pushed in and the table shortened, and Barnes felt his arms pull into his sides. Ruth broke the silence with her declaration about Robert's transience.

Call sat back in his chair at the head of the table. His hands rested flat and motionless, palms cupped on the table top. He pushed a toothpick around in his mouth with his tongue. Barnes finished his chicken fajita, his third, as Ruth began to speak.

"He doesn't want any lifelines. His primary goal in life is to be alone, with only his books. His only office, himself. No lifelines that way. Just read a book and write a paper. Look for life and adventure within the safety of bound pages. Pathetic." She paused for a breath. "He thinks he takes a chance with life with those papers he writes. His greatest goal is to create a new vocabulary, a critical methodology he calls it, that's brand damn new. To him, that's important, that's life. He can't live life or even write about life, he has to write about those who do. Pathetic. Well, to damn with him."

Call offered, sitting forward in his chair and removing the toothpick, "He fails to understand the connections."

"Connections," Ruth echoed. She looked at Call, pressing him forward. Barnes could see that Call wished he had not said anything. But Ruth would not let him retract his words and kept looking at her father.

"You are a lot like your mother," Call said, and all at once Barnes saw in Call's drawn face the face of an old man. "In this light and here in this room, with everything that she picked out for us, you look a lot like her. This table," Call said, running his fingers across the surface. He stopped talking and Ruth did not push him. She allowed him to work into his memory. "We couldn't afford this table, but we wanted it. We saw it downtown, and it was to be the first new thing we owned. And around this table we ate and fought and loved, and we fed you and changed your diapers here because when you came along we had no other table in the house. We scolded you and praised you and helped you learn to read and write here. Right here at this chair that Grace sits in you sat in, and I sat in this chair right next to you while your mother cleaned the dishes and walked by to look over your shoulder and make sure I was doing it right. And where Barnes is sitting is where she sat when she told me that she had cancer. And right here, I can see it like a stain, is where I cried. Those connections."

Ruth stood and walked behind Call. Sparks of light reflected from the tears in her eyes. She stood behind Call, who sat looking at his hands together on the table in front of him, and she kissed the crown of his head, then laid her cheek against it. She stood there for a moment, with her head resting on Call's head and with Call looking silently down at the stains on the table that only he could see.

Barnes felt as though he were eavesdropping on the corners of intimacy and even though he thought of looking away, he watched Ruth embrace her father under the cool yellow light above the table.

Finally and slowly, she lifted her head and kissed Call again, then said, "You're too good, Daddy."

A smile crossed Call's face, pressing lines out from and around his mouth and eyes. Barnes saw in those lines and folds on the old man's face a map of history—mornings and evenings and starless nights, mysteries never unraveled, battles within the walls of that house and wars fought on the foreign soil of another continent, knowledge of the necessary tools needed by the next generation and the questions and fears of how to pass on those tools, connections with a past that was lost other than in him and the acceptance of a legacy he hoped to have formed, exacting fires of love, illnesses and accidents and leavings and returnings and quests and initiations—a breath drawn and a life lived.

"You two go," Ruth said. "I'll clean up this mess." She swept her hand around to indicate the table of dishes and silverware. "You go and discuss your baseball game."

Barnes began to say something, to offer help, to at least cart the dishes into the kitchen, but he was suddenly captured by a tear that traveled down from Ruth's eye. He nodded and followed Call from the room.

They sat in the front room with the television off. Barnes heard a gust of wind push against the windows and looked out to see leaves blowing down the street. As suddenly as the leaves were blown one way, they were blown back. The capricious winds of a cold front.

They sat in large, overstuffed chairs turned at angles to face both each other and the television set across the room. Call sat with a groan, easing himself downward by pressing both hands onto the arms of the chair. He had an unfinished look to him. Even though Call had made his life studying books and histories, Barnes only saw a completeness when the man stood outside with his Stetson shading his eyes and his boots scraping an arc of dirt.

"Windy?" Call asked.

"Front's moving through."

"That so? The game going to get rained out?"

"No, it's a dry front, or so Ed Green said this morning."

"That's good. I like to end a summer day with a baseball game. Life doesn't get a helluva lot better than that; although, I'd rather be down there in the stands where Hurdle can hear me when I yell at him." Call placed his unlit pipe in his mouth and breathed around the pipe's stem as though he were smoking. "Baseball doesn't translate all that well to television. It's not technological to begin with. It doesn't have an MTV sort of quickness, like violent advertising. Baseball is meant for a stadium under the sun and played on grass—you don't have to listen to an announcer tell you about miles-per-hour fastballs caught on the radar gun or a manager who manages with one eye on the computer screen."

"Thank you, Ring Lardner," Barnes said.

"I don't know that Ring Lardner talked in metaphors, but baseball is something like what we wish life were like."

"And how's that?"

"Within all that repetition there exists the constancy for accident. You never know what's going to happen and when it does, you suck up and go to the next inning. The next day, though, begins everything new. Yesterday's score is as important as last week's mail, and in a single swing we can atone for the previous day's strikeout or dropped fly. It's clean and it's clear in that way. Nothing like it. You've got to know that God's a baseball fan."

Grace skipped into the room. She had changed into pajamas with images of ballerinas dancing across her chest and down her legs, and she ran into the room with an airish explosion of delight, running to and jumping on Call's lap.

"Oh-my-God, hija," Call groaned as he encircled Grace within his arms. "You're no longer a light little girl, are you?"

Grace hugged her grandfather and said, "Nope. I'm growing up, aren't I?"

"That you are, darling, and I wish I could stop it."

Grace looked at Call with a singular tilt to her head, considering, it seemed to Barnes, whether her grandfather meant what he had said and whether he could actually keep her from growing up.

Barnes knew, though, what Call had meant. He had no children of his own nor any nephews or nieces, but he had fostered a certain relationship with Call's family. He had first seen Grace when she was less than two days old, her eyes shut tight like a little kitten's as she slept inside the cradle of her mother's arm. He had seen Grace fall from atop the fence, watched her skin both knees when Call took the training wheels off her bicycle, swallowed a choke when she cried after a boy at day care had told her that she was not pretty. He felt that he was as close to her as any person other than Call or Ruth.

He understood why Call hovered over her whenever she played in the park, why he walked past a window every two minutes whenever she played in the yard, why he replaced the short picket fence on the side of the house with a six-foot picket fence. The world, Barnes knew, was not a logical world. One could plan and prepare for the accidents of life, but not for every accident—not for a man toting a rifle through an Asian jungle or for a scolding wind that blows too strong or for an evil.

"Did you kiss Grandpa good-night?" Ruth asked. She leaned against the doorway's frame with her arms crossed. That errant strand of hair fell across her face and she tucked it back behind her ear. She smiled at the scene of her father and daughter in such obvious enjoyment of each other's presence.

Grace said, her eyes squinting and her mouth forced into a tightness, "Grandpa said that he won't let me grow up."

"Well, you tell your grandpa that he can pick up after you from now on, then."

"You making a mess?" Call asked as though he could not believe it.

Grace shook her head but lost her tight face within a smile. Call tickled her side and she laughed and squirmed on his lap.

"Give Grandpa a kiss and say good-night to Barnes," Ruth said. She pushed herself from the door frame and stepped toward Grace.

Grace kissed Call on the cheek and, after crawling from Call's lap, said to Barnes, "Good-night, Barnes."

Barnes said good-night and Grace followed her mother from the room. Barnes could hear Ruth's voice fade as the two ascended the stairs. "You warm enough in those pajamas?" Grace must have nodded. "Teeth brushed?" "All of them?" "What story do you want to hear?" "You want your grandpa to read to you tonight?" "You sure?" "Okay. You crawl into bed and I'll ask him if he'll read a short one to you. But if you want any more than one then I'll read them. He wants to watch baseball with Barnes and anyways I haven't got to read to you all week."

Grace's slight footsteps receded up the stairs while Ruth's turned and grew louder. She stood again in the doorway. "Grace wants you to read to her again tonight," she said. "If you would rather watch the game, then I'll tell her that she'll just have to make do with me."

"Ta bueno," Call said with a smile. "Are you kidding? Read to that young lass or watch television?" Call slapped his knees and rocked forward in his chair. As Call pushed himself from his chair, he said over his shoulder to Barnes, "I'll be back in a whip, Barnes. Don't let those Rockies get too far down." He limped from the room, turning on the television as he passed it and then patting Ruth on the shoulder on his way.

Ruth sat in Call's chair and sighed as she slumped back into the hollows left from Call's body. She closed her eyes and suddenly tightened them as though a galvanic thought had crossed her mind, maybe that she had wrenched her heart in some way or that the way ahead of her that had once opened in light now receded into shades of darkness. With her eyes still closed and her face framed within the folds of her hair, she asked, "You know what I wish, Barnes?"

Barnes had nothing to say but did not want to say nothing. "Peace on earth," he said.

She smiled and shook her head.

"The Rockies would get some starting pitching?"

She shook her head again and laughed a smokey laugh.

"What then?"

"I wish A&W would put their cream soda in those little plastic bottles like Pepsi. It would make such a pretty amber color."

"Wishing for the moon, my dear."

Her voice softened into a whisper then as though they sat together in church, "Aren't we all at times wishing for the moon?"

Barnes did not notice that she had opened her eyes and was looking at him. He had looked at her mouth, at the soft curl of her lips as she spoke, at her words whispering out in sibilant circles.

She said, "We don't get rehearsals in life—the big things happen only once and too often the important part is not what you do but how you deal with what you have done. Daddy and his war, Robert and me, you and that fire. We have to deal with what we've done."

"Or didn't do."

"Or didn't do."

"You sound a good bit like Call."

"I am his daughter, you know, and I can think of a lot worse people to sound like. He has a knowledge that I'd just like to tap into sometime."

"He knows things."

"He knows things," Ruth agreed.

Neither spoke and they sat together in the room within their sphere of silence. The baseball game faded in front of them until the voices of the announcers became distant.

Barnes remembered the view from the lifeless bodies of his crewmembers up toward the helispot where he had waited out the fire's eruption. The hill looked like a ruined cathedral and he had, at every body, kneeled and prayed. He had expected to find an anarchy of bodies discarded like trash along the slope, but they looked calm as if cast in bronze and placed with care along the old fireline. He tried not thinking of them. He tried thinking of anything else, but always remembering his fire. And each night since, his dreams had laid him host to the violent orchestra of that afternoon.

"I miss you sometimes," Ruth said.

Barnes nodded. Sometimes, when he thought about it, he also missed himself. Saying that, however, would have left him hobbled, feeling exposed as even thinking it left him breaking apart.

"Grace said that once to me," Ruth said.

Barnes looked at her.

"She said that you sometimes seem to be away even though you're right here."

"Grace is a perceptive girl for five."

"All kids are perceptive at five. They know a whole lot more than we think. Growing up is a process of unlearning some of the stuff we naturally know."

"Kids are something."

"Children are the only second chance in life. She's my chance." Ruth looked around the room, as did Barnes. Unlike Call's study, this room belonged to more than one person. Photographs of Grace dominated the walls, but in those photographs stood Robert and Ruth and Call. Grace formed the jewel center of each one around which moved the others. Western art hung on the walls which held no photos. Most of them were Taos prints by Gustave Bauman or ranching scenes by Arthur Mitchell, Call's favorite from Southern Colorado. Earth tones, leather furniture, a distressed coffee table, old clocks with heavy hour sounds, a floor ashtray spirited from Denver's Brown Palace Hotel.

When he looked back at Ruth, he could see that she was looking intently at a photograph of her with Grace and Robert, a studio photograph made in black-and-white with the three of them smiling and sitting close together.

She said, "What's funny is that in some ways I do still love Robert, and I don't at all and I won't ever again. All of them at once—it's so damn confusing. I didn't want what my parents had but even more than that, what I really wanted and needed was exactly what they had while my mother was still alive. I knocked myself out running away from that and that was all I ever wanted. Eventually I searched for that. But things don't work out like that anymore, do they? Happy endings."

"Except now for Grace."

Call walked into the room, smiling, cutting off Ruth before she could answer. His gray eyes held steady and clear with a brilliance to them that showed he had seen as much in his one life as most men could only hope for if they lived twice. And that now, after it all, he was happy with his life. Barnes wanted that, what Call had, another couple of decades of decisions and wonder and the very real possibility of a happy ending.

"You two look lost in a conspiracy, sitting here in the dark," Call said.

"Just talking," Ruth answered. She rubbed her eyes with the palm of a hand.

"That's all well and good, but your little girl says she needs a good-night kiss from you."

Ruth nodded. She placed a hand on Barnes's knee to help her stand. She gave her father a kiss on the cheek before mounting the stairs to Grace's room.

Call turned on a floor lamp and sat in his chair. The leather chair exhaled comfortably when he sat. He took his pipe and lit it, puffing peacefully.

"You're going back, I trust," Call said without looking at Barnes.

"Yes," Barnes said.

"All of the questions answered?"

"Not even close."

"They never will be. Trust me on that."

Call took his pipe from his mouth and looked at it. He smiled, "Life ain't always good, you know, but it's far better than the alternative."

"I have to agree with that," Barnes said.

"The good stuff," Call said. He turned and pointed his pipe at Barnes. "You have to remember to remember the good stuff. The bad will always find a way to interrupt your sleep, but the good needs a tad bit of prodding sometimes. You live with the parameters that life gives you. Some stuff you're never going to get past. Some stuff is irrevocable. What you have to do is not let them work you too far down. That day on that fire is one of those days."

Barnes looked at Call. He could see that Call had long ago paid admission to the brotherhood Barnes had recently joined. They held each other's glance for a moment before each looked elsewhere. They remained silent for a long time.

Chapter Five

FRIDAY

From the death of his parents, Barnes had learned that certain moments divide our lives with an uncompromised boundary of past and present, a then and now of singular experience. One of these defining moments happened for Barnes as he walked across the dusty helispot to the edge of the ridge. He stopped there as though he had come to a wall or to a precipice.

Something terrible began to happen then, at first slowly, then compounding in geometric quickness. Everything was coming wrong. When he first noticed the fire, its smoke columned up in distracted spirals, negligible wisps joining earth and sky. Within minutes, though, that immediate world of earth and sky would turn felon.

Barnes saw a hawk on the wing high above the ridge as it pitched nervously in the vectors of wind, fighting against the steep currents to keep itself steady. The hawk dipped one wing to veer off and disappeared as it crossed the opposite ridge. The hawk's erratic flight was Barnes's first clue.

The scent of burning leaves and wood grew strong, and Barnes looked down along the fireline his crew had followed and helped construct. He saw the work they had accomplished, a good three-foot line to mineral soil, a prohibitous scar that he feared would be lost. He imagined them in their movements hours earlier while he rested on the pad awaiting his helicopter shuttle. They would have walked single file, passively, with their heads down and their eyes on the boot heels of the person in front of them like a line of prisoners. Their footsteps deadened within the dust and dirt that floated around their White's boots. Their bodies already tired from the three-week accumulation of sixteen- and eighteen-hour days stacked one on another, blurring distinctions of afternoons and mornings into falling confusions. Walking like dead men walking.

Hunter came up to stand next to Barnes. "It doesn't look good," he said, then cleared his throat a little. "I hope that jumper's mouth didn't write us a check his butt can't cash."

Barnes turned to speak with Hunter. He also cleared his throat as he coughed out the dust he was breathing. He pointed along the ridgeline toward the other helspot. "Okay, listen. Get everybody to H-1. It's larger and a better safety zone."

"You want us to improve the line?"

"No. Just walk along the jumpers' scratch line. Quickly."

Hunter began to say something but stopped himself and walked back to his squad. They had all recognized an urgency, and none were sitting. Barnes watched as Hunter pointed along the ridge and began walking in that direction. Aggie followed Hunter. Behind her, Kapell and George fell into line with Ira and Monterey bringing up the rear, each with a Stihl chainsaw over his shoulder.

Barnes yelled for Kapell and George to drop the cubitainers of water and boxes of MREs that they carried and for Ira to leave behind the Dolmar of fuel and oil. They did so without losing a step.

Barnes looked back down on the fire. A few ash-white flakes floated around him. He reached for his radio to call Chandler but was interrupted by another firefighter walking toward him.

"Heah, Barnes. We could have used you earlier. What kept you?"

"Powell." Barnes reached out his hand. The two men shook. For the first time that afternoon, Barnes felt comfortable. That one firefighter stood with him on the ridge meant the others must be on their way to the top.

After drinking from his water bottle, Barnes said, "They took the helicopter for some tourist VIP who wanted a joyride around the fires. Where you been?" Powell was another smokejumper that Barnes had known for years. They had first met when Powell was a member of the Smokey Bear Hot Shots out of New Mexico and Barnes was a squad leader on the Pike crew. They saw each other on fires about every third year, mostly in the Montana area since Powell, like Max Downey, jumped out of Missoula.

Powell's face was a mask of dirt with sweat lines marking his temples. The bags under his eyes were made darker from the dirt and the shadow tossed by his hardhat. "I been working, man," he said with a smile.

"Since when did you take up working?" With the urgency relieved, Barnes felt good enough to joke a little while he waited for his crew to show.

"Barnes," Powell said, clapping a hand on Barnes's shoulder, "Shit-goddamn, I always put in a double day's work. You know that."

"You down there on the line with my boys?"

"And girls. You got some honeys on that crew of yours."

"Yes. Good people. How was their line?"

"I wasn't digging in with them. I was something of a line-locator-slash-line-scout but I couldn't see enough to be a scout and just flagged the line."

"What are you up here for?" Barnes looked over Powell's shoulder wanting to see Chandler and his crew come walking over the rise.

Powell took off his hardhat and wiped his brow. He said, "I came up here where I might be able to see a little better. But even up here you can't see the active part of the fire. I talked with Max about that this morning."

"Where's Max and my crew?"

"Along the line. That's a helluva digging crew you got there."

"Along the line?"

Barnes dialed his radio to crew net and called Chandler. He spoke calmly to Chandler, both from not wishing to alarm his squad boss as well as from an uncertainty as to whether his own fears were warranted.

He could not see the breath of the wind a thousand feet in elevation above him, could not know that within moments the passing front would exhale a last and bitter blow, a fuming whorl of air that would suck the oxygen from him and the valley he stood above.

Barnes did not know that. But he knew something was wrong. Over two hundred fires had left him with an inchoate sense that the tragic could rest perilously on the wings of the wind.

He talked with Chandler and told Chandler to prepare his people to evacuate their line. He called Max Downey, who was then walking back along the jumpers' unfinished scratch line toward

Chandler's position. Max said he could not feel the wind changing in direction or increasing in velocity, that the front wasn't going to be much more than a lowering of the temperature. Barnes argued.

"It's my fire, Barnes," Max said. He was breathing hard.

"It's my crew and I want them heading out now."

"You want this fire, Barnes? Damnit, do you think you can run this fire better than me? You want this fire?"

"Yes. Now. Double it back up the line to H-2. We'll finish our pissing match there."

"It's still my fire," Max said. "We can tie it off and line out and catch any spots. But if you or your crew can't handle it, then I'll call in some Type-II crew that will."

"Max, damnit, listen to me—"

Downey said something in response but Barnes did not hear him. He drew a quick breath as though he could not believe what was beginning. He slowly exhaled, "God."

As in the instant of a knife stroke, the world turned over. The winds, increasing and swirling on the ridge where Barnes stood, became a whirlwind. For a second, the oak leaves and piñon needles suspended in a sudden absence of wind and then exploded with a rattling percussion.

A rolling mass of air raced into the valley.

The tops of the oaks twirled and bent like grass stubble.

Flames stood out as flags from the trees.

A whirlwind of flame and smoke spiraled a hundred yards above the valley.

The fire spilled across the ridge like mercury.

And up the slope where Chandler and Max Downey and a

dozen others waited, the fire cannonaded as in the chimney of a cabin fireplace.

The temperatures rose by thousands of degrees.

A ragged flag of flame began its run.

"Oh-Jesus-God-All-Mighty," Powell said.

The developing flame showed fire and nature in an essential character—beautiful, ominous, uncontrolled, fully unleashed in ferocity.

Barnes shivered in the heat and did not know that his finger remained keyed on his radio's microphone.

Barnes looked around and saw Hunter walking back toward the helispot where they had landed. He began to yell at Hunter but turned back to see that the fire had spotted below the diamond. He stepped closer to the edge of the ridge and could feel the wind eddying, could feel the wind pushing the fire toward him.

A white hardhat turned a corner, and Warner looked up the slope at Barnes. Barnes saw in slow progression as a handful of firefighters trudged up the fireline. They moved too slowly, weighed down by their packs and tools that they should have already discarded.

"Come on," Barnes yelled, even though he knew they could not hear him.

Warner looked at him. The fire's roar deadened the valley and the ridge. The entire world was composed at that moment of the valley where the fire was and the ridge where a possibility lay.

Warner turned and in that action saw the fire and began to run for the ridgetop. Each person below him also turned and saw and turned uphill again to run for safety. They discarded their tools and some pulled off their packs and threw them and some took their fire shelters from their waist belts and some opened their shelters and began to lie inside them.

Barnes knew the helispot he stood on would not work for a safety zone. Not for a dozen people in their shelters. The helispot was little more than a wide spot on the ridge and the eddying wind would pull the shelters off them in a quick rush of flame.

"Run," Barnes yelled to Powell. "H-1." He pointed along the ridge and both men began running.

Barnes waved and yelled at Hunter as he ran toward them, "Back down H-1."

He came to George, who stood gaping at the blaze racing up toward them. "Run," Barnes yelled, and he grabbed George by the shoulders, almost knocking him down in the process of pushing him forward along the ridge. "Come on."

"Oh God," George said and stumbled a step before Barnes could grab him again and push him upright and toward the helispot.

"Shut up. Stay with me. Run."

The wind blowing on Barnes kept increasing in swells and eddies as he ran. The original blast of wind had subsided but what might have been a gentler gust had increased greatly by the fire's added wind. An increased heat in the fire fed the wind which fed the fire and the fire and the wind fed each other until the fire raced with its own wind across and along and up the ridge. The great mass of heated air pushed the ridge into one flame, tossing branches and ash and dust and burning pieces of wood and leaves high into the air and onto Barnes as he ran and over the ridge's leeward side to start other spot fires which began to burn and race from that side of the ridge up toward the ridgeline where they ran, trapping them between two fires in a match to see which would kill them. The wind swirled and tossed the world as though hit by a tornado and an even deeper roar sent everything in the fire into an absolute silence of sound.

Ahead of him, Barnes could see Powell reach Monterey and both disappeared into a ghost of smoke that shrouded the trail. Barnes swatted an ember that fell on the back of his neck but did not stop running even as he pushed George ahead of him.

They coughed from the smoke, which then lay across the land with a tangible weight. His legs hurt and his lungs fought against him. His eyes teared. And they ran.

Smoke shut the daylight down to a flicker.

Light had turned to darkness which turned amber.

As he ran, Barnes pulled the rolled Nomex shroud inside his hardhat down to protect the back of his neck.

From the brands and sparks and embers falling around him as he ran, Barnes knew the fire had closed on him.

He could not see the fire, only an amber smoke that swirled and shrouded the world into a Pandemonium.

Barnes knew his world would be decided soon. Everything came to that ridgeline and the fire and a helispot he hoped would emerge quickly within the swirling amber.

He ran on, keeping George running also, through the smoke too thick to see through, hoping that he stayed on the ridgetop and had not accidentally run off the side and led himself and George to death.

The ridge opened and Barnes came upon Hunter and the others deploying their fire shelters in the helispot. It looked small, too small, but there was no other choice. They would get hot. They might die. But they had no alternative. Both sides of the ridge were on fire.

Barnes blinked hard, trying to open his eyes through the smoke and ash. Embers burned his face. His heart pounded in his ears, and his thighs began to cramp. He coughed and yelled as he and the others opened their shelters, "Stay in them. Stay in them until we tell you to come out. Don't run. Stay in them."

He tore open the plastic liner to his shelter, pulled out the shelter, shook it open, stepped inside the foot straps, bent and arched his body, and fell to the hot ground, pulling the shelter down on top of him. He scraped a divot in the sand in hopes that some oxygen might pool there. He lay inside the heat of his shelter and listened and panted and coughed. The fire sounded like a waterfall, and then it sounded like he was inside the waterfall.

He said, "GOD." He said it low but he said it in large letters and the single word echoed inside the fire's roar.

He hoped that none of the others in the helispot would panic and run.

Aggie shouted, "We're all right. All right. I'm all right."

Someone answered, "Hang in there."

Someone else, "How long?"

"Hang in there."

"You okay?"

"Yes."

"How long?"

"Just hold tight."

"It's getting hot."

"Hold tight."

"Hang in there."

"Buck up."

"Hail Mary, full of grace—"

Barnes heard an explosion and knew it was a Dolmar and hoped that it lay far enough away that it would not throw fuel onto anyone in the helispot.

Barnes could not think of much but he thought of Lopez and the others whom he knew had died.

He thought of the feel of her body breathing into his as they slept.

His shelter pulled and slapped, and Barnes held tight to the control straps. He hugged the ground. He tried to swallow but could not, and his lips had cracked from the dry heat.

The fire's roar subsided but was replaced by a long hiss, and then the fire roared again.

Barnes lifted the edge of his shelter during a lull and saw smoke and fire brands but no sustained flame. He hoped that the fire had passed them but heard another roar and hugged his shelter back to the ground.

His lungs ached from the smoke and his temples pounded.

A few times its noise lessened, and Barnes thought of raising his shelter but the fire would erupt again as if it were teasing him.

Lying under his shelter, hugging the ground, breathing smoke and dirt, he did not know when it was over. He might have passed out from a lack of oxygen but he was not certain of that either.

He raised the side of his shelter and saw mostly smoke. What remained on fire was now remnant.

He breathed into the ground as though he had held his breath for the time he had spent under the shelter. Suddenly he felt tired, a weariness both palpable and painful.

He lifted his fire shelter and sat up. The wind had begun to clear the fire's smoke and he looked around the helispot at the other fire shelters, all of them covered in dust and cooled embers and looking like insect pods.

A sudden gust of wind blew smoke back down on him.

He pulled his bandanna up to cover his mouth and nose and filter much of the remaining and still thick and suddenly acrid smoke. He coughed, and when the smoke cleared he removed his bandanna and spat. As the smoke cleared around him, he could see and breathe again.

One nightmare had ended and one had just begun.

He tried to speak but could not, so he opened a water bottle, gargled a mouthful, and then drank.

Standing, he felt the weariness again extending along his body. From up the ridgeline, he could still hear the fire's roar, now moving away from them.

"Hunter?" he called. "Powell? Aggie? George? Come on out."

Slowly, each person lifted his shelter and crawled from beneath it. They tested their eyes and stretched and looked at each other with something like embarrassment.

"Everyone okay?" Barnes asked.

Hunter counted. "We're all here." He spat a mouthful of water on the ground.

Barnes looked up at the amber, smoke-stained sun. He said, "Everyone stay put. I'll check on the others."

"I'm going too," said Powell, the jumper. He stepped closer to Barnes.

"It's best if just one person goes down. If I need help, I'll call."

"There's another group of jumpers that were following me up the back side. I'll check on them while you go down the fire-line."

Barnes agreed. He turned to Hunter. "Keep everybody here." He pointed at the helispot as in emphasis. Then he coughed and added, "Make sure they get watered and nobody has shock. Then clear this helispot for the helicopters coming in. They should begin to fly over pretty soon. Eat if you can."

"Okay," Hunter said. His eyes, dark and circular, looked bruised. He said after swallowing, "You sure? You sure you don't want me to go along with you? Aggie can take care of this."

"No. Stay with these guys."

"You're heading for some bad stuff. You sure now?"

"We don't all need to see this."

Barnes turned and walked slowly from the helispot along the trail they had run. He thought they had run a long distance, but they had not. In a fraction of the time it had taken him to run between the two helispots, he walked the distance.

Powell walked behind him and when they reached H-2, they stopped before splitting up. The ground was hot on their boots. Neither man spoke. Each searched the slope first with quick, darting eyes, then a slow concentration to assemble an image of the day's events. They both saw the first body on the slope below them.

"We can check on this line later," Powell said. "Why don't we check on the other jumpers over the hump here?" He pointed in the direction Barnes had seen Powell walk from an hour earlier.

"No. Only one of us needs to go down here. You get the others to the helispot with Hunter."

Powell started to walk off, and Barnes added without looking, "But thanks, man."

"You be careful." And Powell disappeared over the hump in the ridge which had earlier been covered in oak brush but was then a rise of charred and ashen stubble.

The world had turned over and he felt for a moment that he stood above someplace different, that he stood above some landscape he had never before seen and that he stood there without any compass to provide direction.

For an age, he stared like an idiot at the first body not even a hundred feet from where he stood. Then he stepped cautiously from the ridgetop toward the lost people lying like blackened and unstrung pearls on the slope below him.

Barnes had never experienced feelings so cold and controlling and absolute before, nothing before like this frozen stab of truth. Not when his father had died in a hospital bed in front of him nor when his mother had died from a cancer a thousand miles away. His stomach tightened as he walked, and then his neck constricted and he could not swallow the bilious taste in his mouth.

Warner looked to Barnes as though he had knelt in prayer. He faced uphill, both of his feet were on the ground, as were his knees and hands, his forehead was touching the ground as though he had been caught in the act of prayer, a water bottle lay unmelted and with the water still in it within reach of his body, an empty bottle was six feet below him, his hardhat had been thrown by the fire's wind a dozen feet away and had only partially melted, the painted red feather on the hardhat had drained in color across the white plastic, his aramid shirt and pants had burned off except around his waist and torso where they were covered by his daypack, charred strips of his crew T-shirt poked out in a ragged line from the sides of his fire shirt, the laces of his boots had burned but the boots remained essentially okay, frayed strands from his socks ringed the tops of his boots, and he lay with his feet and hands and knees and forehead touching the ground and facing uphill and Barnes remembered him looking up the slope and turning to see the fire begin its run and turning back to begin his own run to where Barnes stood watching.

The bottom of his daypack had burned open and Barnes could see the polyethylene liner surrounding Warner's fire shelter. Where it had been exposed to the passing heat and flames, the liner had only partially melted, but the shelter would never have been of any use, not tucked into the bottom of his daypack like that. He could never had retrieved the shelter in time. Maybe if it were on his waist belt but not from the bottom of his daypack.

One of Warner's hands, his left hand, was still inside its glove. Both had shrunk to half their size. His watch had melted into the charred skin of his left wrist and the surrounding ground.

Barnes looked again at the unmelted water bottle and the scattered tufts of unburned grass and leaves around the body. He knew that Warner might have lived had he used his shelter, had Barnes checked his shelter that morning.

Warner was twenty-four years old, a good man who had died violently at a very young age. This was to be his last fire season before entering law school and eventually joining his father and uncles and cousins in a practice in Denver. A last song of youth before growing up and taking on the responsibilities of a real job.

Warner was a Republican who hated most Republicans but he had grown up Republican and had always voted Republican and knew he would eventually marry a Republican girl, even though he dated mostly girls who were Democrats because, as he had told

Barnes one Friday afternoon over his third marg down at the Rio, "I want to have a little fun first." He had come to fire by accident, filling out the application on a whim and then, because he had broken up with his first Republican girlfriend when she could not accept his interest in girls who were Democrats and because Barnes called the next day expressing an interest in a marathon runner with advanced first-aid training and offered him a job, he became a hot shot firefighter.

That was four years earlier when Warner had joined the Red Feather Hot Shots as one of only two true rookies along with Dago. He nearly peed his pants the first time he saw a good hot flame front up Twenty-Five Mile Creek near Lake Chelan, Washington. He was scared that first time and, like most other firefighters, he remained a little afraid. But he was a fighter. His health was good, his body tall and strong. His will and his interest excellent. Warner had hoped that one day, one day before he left firefighting, he would be tested.

Barnes fingered the button on his radio. Voices moved from the receiver yet were silenced within the echo of soundless air swirling around him, displaced by him as he walked from body to body as though entering the dead-air depths of a tunnel, each step removing him farther from the light, his eyes adjusting and readjusting to the darkness and him praying he would not be able to see that which he saw.

He looked down the fireline for a long time. The sun warmed his back, and the remnants of that afternoon's wind tossed errant eddies around his boots. The world paused and waited. He walked to the next body.

From Warner to Doobie and Stress next to each other seventy-five feet below Warner, to Horndyke close to them, to Lopez alone and curled into herself, to Freeze almost embracing a smokejumper named Fleming whom Barnes did not know, to Earl and Hassler together, to Budd still holding on to his chainsaw, to Sully to Dago to Max Downey to Chandler at the bottom of the line nearly three hundred feet from the ridgeline and within a hope of the diamond area that was not a safety zone after all.

More even than the sight of their bodies, he remembered the smells. The odor of burnt flesh still gagged him, and he remembered looking on and smelling them. At night, in his sleep, it was their sight that haunted him, but during the daylight he inhaled the hovering smell.

Call sat in a wicker chair facing Barnes, who leaned against the porch railing. Call had heard the story before, but he listened again, knowing from his own life that healing is often possible only in the telling of the tale. Call's pipe perched easily and unlit from the corner of his mouth as he watched Barnes speak.

Barnes said, "I realized something then. I realized that nature is indiscriminate. I realized how easily the tragic happens. I don't know that I learned anything other than that." He paused. "Is that what I should have learned?"

"This wasn't a lesson for you," Call said. He filled his pipe with tobacco and tapped the tobacco tight inside the bowl of his pipe. "It wasn't done for your understanding."

Barnes nodded.

Call struck a match on the seam of his jeans. Barnes watched the slight tremor to the man's hands, lined and scarred with road maps of life. Call had been born on his family's ranch in North Park. He had lived a good life. He went to college and became an apprentice scholar and then a warrior in Vietnam and then a university teacher and historian and then a father and grandfather.

Call's hands had met the springs which began the Poudre River, had known wheat stalks rising into the sun, had known dry earth and wet soil. They escorted him and reached out to share him with others. They caught the wind and tested the river and scraped the dirt. They knew the past and offered a faith in their embrace for the future. Years earlier in their first handshake, Barnes knew that in Call was a man he would like. His hand pulsed with life when they shook.

"After we have made our histories," Call breathed, "we have to learn to live with them, to grow at ease with them. We need to become at ease with our lives and our dead."

"But I still keep thinking something."

"And you'll keep thinking something until it drives you crazy. Believe me, I know. You didn't send people up on that ridge to be killed, but I did. I know all those somethings you keep thinking."

Barnes let out a breath. "Max Downey's father wants me to testify that his son didn't do anything wrong."

"Did he?"

"Yes. As much, at least, as anyone else."

"He wants you to lie?"

"No. He believes his son was a good man, and he was. But he wants something official that says so."

"What are you going to do?"

"I can't testify for him. Not because I don't want to lie for his son's sake but because he needs to understand that a lot of people, myself included as well as Max, did some wrong things. If anything positive is to be taken from this, then we all, Max and I and others, have to shoulder our burdens."

"No one to blame?"

"No one to blame and everyone to blame," Barnes said. He looked from Call to the planter Ruth and Grace had weeded earlier in the week. There was no longer any freshness to the turned soil but all of the weeds had been gleaned from the flower bed. A six-inch strand of snow-on-the-mountain lay limp in the grass near the planter.

"You going to keep doing this?" Call asked. He puffed on his pipe and looked through the column of smoke at Barnes.

"Do what?"

"Keep fighting fires?"

"Can't sing or dance," Barnes said. "The funny thing about this job is that I'm fulfilling a prophecy in doing it." He waited for Call to tilt his head in anticipation before explaining. "In high school one day I was working on my car, trying to work on my car, actually, because I wasn't fixing anything. Didn't even know exactly what was wrong. My father comes out of the house, pulling on his jacket and mumbling to himself. Within twenty minutes he had the problem fixed and the hood shut. Before he walked back inside, he turned to me and said, and I remember this distinctly. He said that I'd never amount to a thing if I couldn't fix my own car, that the best I'd do in life is to be a ditch digger. And, by God, that's just what I do on the fireline."

"Goddamn," Call said and raised himself from the wicker chair. "But aren't we feeling sorry for ourselves tonight?"

Barnes fought the sudden heat of anger. He liked Call as much as any man he had ever met and did not want his words just then to form a gap between them, so he stood and breathed steadily but did not take his eyes from Call's.

"You think I'm just feeling sorry for myself?" Barnes asked evenly.

"What I think you're doing is what I did a long time ago after my war. You're trying to impose a reason, a theoretical or meta-physical or theosophical reason for what happened. A chaos hap-pened and you need an order to apply to it. But, son, there isn't one. . . . Yes, I think you're feeling sorry for yourself. What I really think, though, is that what happened on that fire, on that hill, on that day gone bad, is either going to make you a god-damn good man or it's going to break you. Right now you're tee-tering on the precipice, a hazardous place to stand, and you'll go one way or the other. You'll either fall or you'll step away. It's up to you, son."

Barnes smiled in spite of himself. "Give it to me straight, Call. Don't hold back now."

"Barnes, you're demanding a perfection in a world that is too imperfect. I know. I've been there. I have lived my adult life in the shadow of 1965. I have lived my life knowing how easy it would be to let my past rule my future. If I had let that happen, I would not have Ruth or Grace. I would not have had a life at all. That does not mean that I still don't wake up in the middle of the night. It means that I have tried to be the best man that I can. That's your choice, son. That's your choice."

Call tapped Barnes on the shoulder. "It's a helluva cross you're carrying and damn soon you'll need to let it down." He stretched his back and walked inside his house.

Barnes hesitated for a moment before following. He let the screen door swing shut, then opened it again and trailed Call into the front room where Ruth sat wiping a tear from her eye.

Before his eyes completely adjusted to the room's light, he heard Call ask, "What's wrong, sweetheart?"

Ruth answered, "Robert called. I just finished talking with him."

Barnes saw Call's hands ball into fists and work in those fists as though kneading his palms. A coldness invaded the room.

Ruth wiped her eyes again and tossed her head back to throw her hair away from her face. She blinked hard a couple of times and sniffed and held her chin high and forward, and Barnes could just hear Call as a young man telling his baby daughter with the scraped knee to "buck up."

But Call said nothing to his daughter.

Ruth continued, "He said that he wouldn't be back home for a while. That he needed to figure some things out. That he still loves me, but he just needs to figure out some things."

"I don't know what to call it, but that sure as hell isn't love," Call said. He sat next to his daughter and took her in his arms.

Ruth laid her head in the hollow of Call's shoulder.

"You okay, Mommy?" Grace asked. She stood next to Barnes in the room's doorway. She was dressed for sleep in her ballerina pajamas, and she held a tattered blue blanket about the size of a large pillow, her "Gi-Gi" she called it. She stood pigeon-toed next to Barnes with an uncertainty. With one hand she held the Gi-Gi to her face, and with the other she reached out to hold on to the pocket of Barnes's jeans, waiting for some sign from her mother.

"Oh, baby," Ruth said. She turned to hold her arms wide for Grace to walk into. "I'm okay, just a little sad is all."

Grace walked into Ruth's arms, and they hugged each other.

"Everything's okay, sweetie, everything's okay," Ruth said. She rocked from side to side with Grace, swaying to a silent melody only the two of them could hear. "Everything's okay. You're all ready for bed?"

Grace stood a step back from Ruth and said, "Yes, except I can't reach the medicine jest."

"The medicine chest?"

"Yes, that. I need to brush my teeth, and I'm too short to reach my toothbrush. God made me that way."

"And He did a damn good job at that," Call said.

"Daddy," Ruth said.

Call pushed himself from the couch. "I'll help you out, little lady." He took Grace's small hand in his own and walked with her. The white of her tiny hand, soft and white as a cloud, shown in bright relief against the red clay color of Call's hand, like thin air above adobe.

Barnes let them pass and begin to climb the stairs before he moved to take Call's place next to Ruth. Her eyes were rimmed and shaded in darkness, and Barnes understood that she had wrestled often with this problem. Her hands stayed in motion, moving from her knees to her face in search of some comfort.

Barnes reached over and placed his hand on Ruth's shoulder and she leaned into him. He breathed in the smell of her, a scent rich in poignancy and subtlety. He liked the smell so much that he smiled as he breathed.

After a few seconds, she pushed herself away from Barnes and reached to turn off the floor lamp beside the couch. Then she returned to his embrace, and they remained that way well into the night. Barnes felt his arms begin to ache and want for stretching, and the muscles of his legs knotted. Still, he held her as he watched the shadows cast by the lights of passing cars stretch along the walls behind her. He liked watching shadows that were only shadows.

Chapter Six

SATURDAY

Midnight was bathed in moonlight. Barnes rolled from his bed and stood to peek through the blinds of his bedroom window. At first, he felt a slight chill standing so close to the glass. He lifted the window and smelled the breeze, the air so clear it tasted fresh as a stream. The world shimmered in the remnants of the light May rain that had wet the grass and street. The rain, however, had left and the sky had cleared. The moon shone high and clean and the midnight sky was jeweled with stars.

Somewhere from down the road, Barnes could hear someone singing. A tenor sang the scales, running up and down in succession for five minutes. The singer stopped. The night became loud in the absence of his music.

A bat flew in the tenuous ring of light cast from the lamppost across the street. The bat swooped and dove for insects attracted to the light, the light becoming both their quest and their death.

He searched the world, and in the sudden absence of sound and of cars driving along the street and of people walking from campus and in the world washed momentarily clean, he found a vacancy—silent and clear as an iced lake.

Barnes sat back on his bed. He lay again with his head on his pillow, no covers on him, his feet barely apart and his arms crossed on his chest. He let tracings of the night's wind bathe him in cool waves.

He remembered Maria Lopez, could still remember the feel of her lips on his. He still carried the touch of her fingers cool and light on his skin. He wished he could touch her face one more time.

He stared at her eyes. In their innocent gaze, her eyes teased under the brown-black bangs which covered her forehead. As deep as the night, he always thought when he looked at her, the flashes of light bouncing from her eyes like wafers of moonlight on a midnight lake.

He closed his eyes and dreamed that she lay next to him, her black hair soft as a whisper on his arm. That she rolled into him to wrap her leg over his. That he nestled his face in the warmth of her neck, smelling the hint of lavender in her perfume. He did not love her, although he had felt it was something very close to that and might have eventually become that, and he wondered whether she had felt anything similar.

They shared the winter between two fire seasons and as that second season approached, the summer that would be her last, she told Barnes that they would have to break up for the season. She did not want anyone to think that she was on the crew because she had slept with the crew boss. When the season ended, she said as they stood together in the tempered light of dusk, they would talk. That May afternoon on his porch, she told him that she would give up a lot for him, but she would not give up herself. Then she said to him, "Mi corazon," and kissed him softly on the lips.

He woke at two o'clock. The side of the bed where she would have been was empty.

Barnes turned on the radio to a repeat broadcast of a talk show aired the previous afternoon. He listened for a minute to a fat man who made over twenty million dollars a year tell some woman from North Dakota how he understands the needs of the people of this country so much better than her, or anyone. "No," he began. "Just listen to me. Let me tell you." Barnes wondered when the last time was, if ever, that the man with a voice like a soft doughboy had busted a blister. Stroking Willie in the bathroom would have been about it, he decided. He shut off the fat man.

At six-thirty in the morning he did what he used to do at six-thirty in the morning, what had once formed his morning ritual. He boiled water for a press of coffee, poured a glass full of orange juice, warmed two breakfast rolls in the microwave, and let his mind and body and eyes prepare for the day.

Through his dining room window, he could see Tri-pod perched on his single back leg on the fence that separated his yard from Ruth's. The three-legged squirrel nibbled on a peanut, held tight in his grasp, that Barnes had dotted the fence with earlier in the week.

Barnes gave the squirrel a thumbs-up. "Good man," he said.

He looked at his refrigerator door where he kept photographs and notes and newspaper clippings magneted like pieces of a puzzle. He found in the cluster of things on the door a snapshot of Chandler and Aggie and Warner and half a dozen other crewmembers at last year's end-of-training party, food filling his dining room table, bottles of beer and empty shot glasses littering the table and window sills behind. Lopez and Budd sat leaning into each other on the bench against the room's far wall, their eyes, like those of everyone's in the photograph, at half mast. Kapell held his bottle of Fat Tire beer out toward the camera as in a toast. Horndyke laughed at something Doobie said.

Barnes shut his eyes tight as though he could strangle his thoughts in that way, but they, like the photograph, hung with him.

When Barnes opened his eyes, he saw them again.

Chandler led the way. Behind Chandler as he walked into the dining room to sit silently on the radiator, came the line of ghosts who greeted Barnes each morning. At the end of that line of ghosts, Barnes saw Warner who had died closest to the safety of the ridge, who had died with his head and arms and knees touching the ground as though he were praying.

They sat with steady patience, monuments staring at grief. Their shoulders and arms touched and their hands hung loose between them, their heavily booted feet flat and slightly apart, their clothing the yellow shirts and green pants of their firefighting clothes. The unfolding light of morning backlit them against the room's windows. Their eyes were ice. As he searched each for the scars they wore, Barnes thought that he should be one of them, maybe that he already was.

"After something like that you have two choices—you can live your life either naked or dead."

"Sounds something like a catch-22. And you're damned regardless. If you get yourself back together, somebody'll think you didn't care enough. If you don't get it together, then you cared too much and it kills you."

"Another burden added to all of those things you already carry."

"And a thin line to walk."

"Thin and red as a fireline, but it may be the only way to get any peace in your time."

The Forest Service had hired a psychiatrist to assist Barnes and the remainder of his crew through their grief. An hour before the sun set and while the bodies still lay on the hill to be photographed and charted and measured and examined, the psychiatrist stood looking at Barnes and the survivors from the front of the hotel meeting room. The psychiatrist stood with one hand on the hip of his Dockers. His other hand loosely held a pair of eyeglasses dangling from his long, thin fingers.

Barnes watched those fingers move when the man talked. How they took flight when the man stressed a point. How they fluttered like doves. How he sometimes seemed to notice how Barnes watched them and then would trap them inside the pockets of his pants. Eventually, though, they would take flight again and the long, thin fingers like the wings of a soft bird would flutter about in front of the man's face.

The man kept his distance from the firefighters. At first, Barnes thought the psychiatrist might have smelled death or fear on them, then he realized that the man smelled the pungent odor of a dozen people who had not taken a real shower for weeks and had not changed their clothes for almost as long, and had been bathed in smoke and dirt as well as the death and fear.

The psychiatrist walked across the room, traversing the front as though caught on a line, telling them about the stages of grief that they would encounter. He never loosened his tie nor did he roll up the sleeves of his white shirt.

As the man walked and talked in front of him, Barnes could feel himself tighten. He felt his fingers rub the muscles of his thigh, and the back of his neck went very rigid. He sat in the front row of the room and could not see how the others were reacting but he could feel their tense response to a man who had read a lot of books about dealing with death.

Barnes heard very little of what the man said. He was still on the hill. He could watch the turmoil surround him and the clouds and the column mix into a hovering presence and the land boil on the edge. And he saw again Warner, who had died nearest the top of the ridge, bent as though praying like an anchorite lost in ashes.

They might have been with the psychiatrist for an hour or two or more, and by the time they left the meeting room for the hotel bar the sun had fallen and the world was dark. Nobody spoke as they walked from the room, nobody even looked another in the eyes. They left with a blindness and muteness that stranded each.

The heavy padding of their boots on the hotel's carpeting echoed distantly in the fluorescent silence. Barnes stood for a minute at a corridor window to look out on the darkness. Aggie passed him, she reached out to quickly and gently grasp his hand. Just as quickly, she turned his hand loose as she continued down the hallway, never looking at Barnes.

"Do you good to have a beer with us, unwind some and maybe help you get to sleep." Hunter had walked up next to Barnes in the corridor and placed his hand on Barnes's shoulder.

Barnes did not turn to look at Hunter. He shook his head and said, "I'll be by in an hour or so. I have another meeting with the investigation team."

Hunter coughed from the minor case of bronchitis he had been carrying for half the season. He said, "At least they know what they're talking about."

Barnes grunted, "If that shrink thinks he knows what's best for us, he'd buy rounds for the night and let us fight out our pain."

Hunter nodded. "You'll stop by before you hit your bed?"

"Just as soon as I'm done with this meeting."

Hunter began to walk away, stopped and turned back to Barnes. "Don't let them pin this on you, Barnes. It wasn't you that caused this."

Barnes nodded but did not answer. He continued to stare out the window while Hunter walked down the corridor. In the distance, Barnes could hear the music of a jukebox.

Barnes knew some of the investigation team members only by reputation, some through fire assignments and some not at all. Barnes shook all of their hands as they each expressed their condolences and grief before the questions began. The questions, prefixed by the team leader's statement that they were not out to hang anything on anyone but to find the truth, were primarily technical. They discussed the weather reports, the red flag warning that was not passed on, the reconnaissance flight, the fire size-up, the fuels, the topography, the strategy for attack, the diamond as a safety zone, the ridge as a safety zone, the communication between firefighters, the strength of a chain-of-command structure.

They talked for three hours and Barnes felt a certain relief from having talked about the fire with people who would have some understanding. They all shook hands again and told Barnes that he would have to stay in Craig for a few more days, his crew would stay at least through the next day when they would be debriefed, but he might have to stay longer.

Besides the blare of the jukebox, the first sound Barnes heard on entering the hotel bar was that of two bodies striking each other at some measure of force. The slap of skin followed by a blasting exhalation like that of two great bellows and then George screaming, "I got you, you bastard. Any takers?"

Barnes stood for a moment to allow his eyes to adjust to the darkness. Then he looked into the bar with some disbelief. Aggie sat at a table nearest him, her shirt sleeve rolled up, a pile of dollar bills in front of her and her hand engaged in an arm-wrestling battle with some male firefighter off another crew. George, stripped of his shirt and with his chest a hard pink, crouched outside a makeshift ring of tables as another firefighter readied himself for some sort of punk-sumo-mosh pit wrestling match. They ran at each other, leaped in the air, and slapped their chests together. The one who landed on his feet and within the ring was the winner. Hunter and Kapell and Ira sat at the bar with a row of shot glasses in front of them, some still full. Kapell tossed one down and shouted as loud as the weather's wind. Ira set a match to the drink in his shot glass, lighting it on fire before downing it and shouting to match Kapell's yell. Hunter laughed drunkenly, almost slipping from his bar stool. Monterey stood in a corner of the room next to the jukebox, nursing a pint and smiling at the saturnalia taking place on the floor between him and Barnes. A yellow-shirted woman from the Pike Hot Shots dropped four quarters into Monterey's pint glass. He fished them out and dropped them in the jukebox's coin slot, playing first George Thoroughgood's "Bad to the Bone."

Barnes had expected to find his crew passed out in grief, walking car wrecks, frail and shaking uncontrollably as though they had been stripped naked and stood in a cold snow. He expected to find them apart from humanity. He expected to see them sitting in the cool wind of the bar's air conditioner with the soft flutter of the hotel's other patrons surrounding them in the dark. He expected them to be overfilled with self-pity and a fiction that life should have no miseries such as what they knew now so intimately.

Instead, there were no other patrons in the bar besides his crew, the handful of jumpers who had been on the lee side of the hill with Powell, and part of the Pike Hot Shot crew and a helitack crew and local BLM firefighters who had helicoptered to the ridge soon after the fire passed over in the vague hope that they might be able to help someone do something.

Barnes walked to the bar and sat next to Hunter.

Hunter closed his left eye to look at Barnes. He said, "I only see two of you this way." He drank the last of his whiskey and called to the bartender, "Barkeep, another for me and something here for my buddy. What'll you have, Barnes?"

The bartender stood in front of Barnes. A wisp of blonde hair fell across her eyes and the way she pushed it back in place behind her ear reminded Barnes of someone.

"What do you have on tap?" asked Barnes, watching the woman's movements, watching the tips of her slender fingers push a coaster in front of him and how she wet her lips before speaking.

"They got Fat Tires," Kapell interrupted, leaning over Hunter and almost knocking him into Barnes.

"I'll take one of those," Barnes said to the bartender.

She nodded and drew a pint of the beer for Barnes. It overflowed and ran in amber rivers down the side of the glass and dropped on the bar top as she placed it on the coaster in front of Barnes.

"This on the doctor also?" she asked and smiled.

Before Barnes could answer, could ask her what she meant, Hunter slurred, "Yes. The doc's picking it up tonight. A damn good man, that shrink."

"To the doc," offered Ira in toast. Hunter and Kapell raised their glasses to meet Ira's. "To the doc," they both said.

"He must have one helluva nice expense account," the bartender said as she walked to the bar's other end to serve Powell and another jumper.

Barnes looked at Hunter. He felt the question forming in his mouth also wrinkle his brow. Before asking, though, he needed that first cool sip of beer.

Hunter yawned, "He said he was here to help us." He took a drink from his shot glass. "And you said that if he really wanted to help us that he should buy rounds." He took another drink. "And so's I put two and two together and agreed with you, Barnes."

"And everyone is charging to him?"

"Not everyone. Just us and the jumpers. The others have to pay their own way."

"And what do you plan on doing tomorrow when he doesn't pay up?"

Hunter leveled his voice and spat, "Fuck him. Fuck him and his steps to recovery and his grieving process and his fucking limp wrist."

"Yeh," said Kapell, again leaning hard into Hunter. "Fuck the fucking fucker."

"All right." Barnes drank from his beer. It tasted better than he thought it should.

White, who had been sitting by himself at a corner table and who should have died on the hill instead of Lopez, walked over to stand between Barnes and Hunter. "Barnes," he said, "we have to talk."

His skin had drained to a shallow pall and his fingers shook where they held on to the bar. Unlike any of the others from Barnes's crew who had gathered in the bar, White did not carry any burn blemishes or scrapes or heat discolorations on the skin of his hands or face. He tried holding Barnes's eyes but could not and looked down at the bandage on the back of Barnes's hand covering a burn received during the run.

Barnes felt the muscles along his jaws tighten and blood rush through his eyes and ears. He took hold of his beer glass and said, "We have to talk, but not tonight." He breathed hard and felt a red heat burn behind his eyes. He continued, "What I'm going to do is take a drink from my beer and if you're still standing there when I put the glass back down, I'll kick your ass."

He did not wait for White to answer but drank a long, full pull from his beer, and when he replaced the glass, White had left.

"He ain't such a bad guy," Hunter said with surprising lucidity.

Barnes flashed in anger toward Hunter but restrained himself. "No, but I just didn't need to deal with him right now."

"Lopez didn't die because of White, you know. White has that to live with, though. He'll carry that weight with him for a good long while. But he couldn't have known."

"I know that. But I still don't know if I can . . ." He let his sentence trail off. "I don't know."

In the middle of his beer, Barnes began watching the bartender again. She seemed leashed to the beer taps, looking at him and smiling from time to time and then returning to the taps to fill another pint. He watched her fingers move with grace and subtle strength and he watched her eyes as they surveyed the bar and crossed his looking back at her. Her face was soft and white. The hair somewhere between blonde and cornsilk and long enough to be held in a knot behind her neck, except for the errant strand that kept falling across her face. Barnes continued to watch her while he drank his beer.

When she noticed that his glass was empty, she asked if he needed another.

He nodded and said that he did.

She filled it. As she placed the pint in front of him, she said, "I'll get this one."

"Thank you."

She smiled and Barnes met her smile with his own.

She leaned across the bar and said, "I heard what happened on that fire. That's terrible. I don't see how you can do it, fight fire. That's just too scary."

"Sometimes," Barnes said. "Sometimes, but not often. It's usually pretty simple stuff." He could think of little else to say that could say anything at all.

Kapell, however, leaned forward and said, filling his voice as full of Chandler as he could, "If you want to die in bed, don't become a hot shot."

"Fuckin'-A," George said from behind. He had put his shirt back on, but a trickle of blood ran from the corner of his mouth.

The bartender smiled again and left.

"I made me fifty dollars," Aggie said, leaning heavily into Hunter's back. She tossed a wadded ball of bills onto the counter, then turned around and surveyed the crowd of firefighters. "Shit-all-mighty, there isn't a good-looking piece of meat in this bar. I need me some blinders."

She pushed away from the bar in the general direction of the jukebox. She walked as though she was maneuvering through a maze, circling tables and staggering from side to side with unsteady grace. She scanned the musical offerings, her head and body bobbing and swaying with absolutely no discernible beat. After finding what she wanted, she plugged in the numbers and stood back to wait for the song to begin. Two songs later, during which she stood and watched the room with predatory concentration, Percy Sledge's "When a Man Loves a Woman" slid across the bar's dance floor. Aggie followed the music and found a man off the Pike crew to dance with. She buried her face in his neck and Barnes could see her head move in sobbing convulsions.

That song ended and Flogging Molly captured the dance floor with "What's Left of the Flag." Aggie wiped her eyes and tossed her body into the song. The dance floor filled. Even Ira and Kapell stumbled from their seats to find somebody to dance with.

Halfway into the song, Ira flung himself to the dance floor and began to flop on his back. Kapell joined him, and the two finished the dance with what they called the hot tuna.

The wake oscillated between gloom and joy, a ride and tie of tears of laughter. An hour after last call, with the beer taps shut off and all of the bottles stored in boxes and a threat from the local police chief, Barnes finally shoved the last of his people out of the bar.

"You need someone to talk to?"

Barnes looked at the blonde bartender. "All I've been doing is talk since the fire."

He started to walk away.

She said, "We don't have to talk."

They made love in the shower with his body pressing against hers and him holding her by the curve of her butt against the shower's wall tiles. The water, as hot as he could stand it, pelted his back, and the steam surrounding them while they engaged cast the shower stall in a swirling fog. They made love again in the bed with her on top, her back arching and him reaching to embrace the round of her breasts. She folded herself back onto his chest and remained there for a long time after he had gone soft and slid from her body. She left an hour before sunrise, kissing him softly on the forehead and lips after dressing in the room's darkness while he silently watched.

After she left him, Barnes stayed awake. He wished that he could wake up and be over with his nightmares, but knew that it was only his dreams that had been lost. He wondered why he had not cried and why he had not punched someone or something or why he had not yet drunk himself into a stupor.

As he lay with the covers bunched around him and the sun's morning light spreading across the room, his ghosts first came to him. They spread in a cloistral circle around the foot of his bed and watched his eyes swell with recognition at the advent of his dead.

Chandler might have been the first of them to die, but dying only a matter of seconds before the others perished. He was the farthest down of Barnes's crew and as their leader he would have been the first in and the last out. His full name was Walker Chandler and he had come to the Red Feather Hot Shots after a year of heli-tack in Yellowstone and two years on the Entiat Hot Shots. Twenty-eight years old, a college degree in sociology and an interest in eventually joining the FBI. He stood on the left of the circle naked except for the left sleeve of his shirt from elbow to wrist which was charred ocher.

If Chandler could have talked, he would not have forgiven Barnes, for there was nothing to forgive Barnes for. Events decide themselves, Chandler might have said, and that is the mystery

Barnes could not know. Even in his sublimity, Chandler could not offer absolution nor could he tell Barnes of the simple acts of expiation. He could not answer "Why?" A fire, he might have wanted to say, is dynamic. It cleanses some and destroys others.

The sun continued to light the room until the ghosts were removed. And when Barnes saw them the next morning and every morning following, Chandler, like the others, was recast without the charred body Barnes prayed over on the ridge.

Barnes spent Saturday evening arranging his war bag, making certain that everything he needed for the coming fire season would find its place. It formed a ritual that he took comfort in, something similar to a homecoming. He ticked through the mental list of necessities, from the seven pairs of new cotton socks to the extra vitamins. He first laid everything on the floor to inspect it before putting it in its proper stuff sack.

With The Mavericks on his stereo offering songs from paradise to hell, Barnes filled the backpack that served as his summer home. He then checked his line gear. For a moment he felt the presence of his ghosts observing him as he removed his new fire shelter from its bag and fingered the plastic wrapping protecting it.

He oiled all three pairs of White's loggers, his primary pair in their second season and his two backups, both of which had been reworked at the White's shop in Spokane. He chose three sets of Nomex fire clothes from his private stash. Over the years he had collected a dozen old-style shirts and would not part with them. The new polyester-looking shirts did not suit him well at all, so he kept his own. He rolled and taped two sets of shirts and pants for his war bag, and folded a third set on top of his line gear.

Just before eleven o'clock, the telephone rang, startling Barnes as he sat on the front room floor surrounded by his equipment.

"Barnes, pick up." Ruth's voice was edged and erratic.

He felt a cold deadening as she said that Grace was missing. At first she spoke unhesitatingly, stringing the words together in mercurial quickness, and then slower a second time as though transferring her words.

He knew he said something in response and that she answered him, but exactly what he could not say. He hung up the telephone and stood for a protracted second inside the silence of his house. An echo beat and beat again before he left for Ruth's home next door.

Ruth met him at the front door. Taking him into her arms as though pulling in a lifeline, she held him tight to her. Barnes returned the embrace.

"Have you called the police?" he asked as he stepped back from her.

"They're on their way." She turned and walked into the kitchen.

"And Call?" Barnes asked as he followed.

"He's already started looking for her, going to the neighbors' houses to get some help."

"Good. Tell me what happened." In the light of the kitchen, Barnes could see how purple and swollen her eyes had become from crying. He wanted to hold her again, rock her inside the embrace of his arms, but he also knew that could wait until a balance was restored.

Ruth swallowed hard and inhaled her tears. "I went to say goodnight before going to bed and she was gone. And so was Harp."

"No idea where?"

"None."

"She didn't say anything earlier about anything?"

"No. Nothing."

"Did you call Robert?"

"He's in Denver and said to call him back as soon as we hear anything."

"He's not driving up?"

She did not say anything.

"Okay, tell me which way Call went and I'll go another."

"Down Mountain toward downtown," she said, lifting a trembling finger to point through a window into the darkness.

"I'll go up Loomis and wake people to help us look. Stay here in case she returns."

Ruth nodded her head quickly, her clenched eyes tight as her body. She leaned her weight back against the counter. "Oh, God," she said, covering her eyes. "Dad told me tonight that he's dying. I can't lose them both. He's my past and she's my future. I can't lose them both. Please." She reached out for him.

Barnes took hold of her shoulders but did not embrace her. He bent to see her fallen eyes and said, "We'll find her. I promise we'll find her."

He left quickly, wishing he could hug her into him but not wanting to spend another moment not searching for Grace.

From around the corner came the sound of cars stopping on hard pavement, the soft tramping of shoes jogging to Ruth's front door, a knocking followed by the retreating voices of the police as they entered Ruth's home.

He ran from house to house, knocking on each loud enough for someone to come to the door, a woman in her robe and a man holding a pistol in his hand. He asked each person he woke to dress and go to Ruth's house to help the police in their search. He looked down the alleys caught inside barriers of darkness and cursed the limits of his vision. All he could see was darkness and nothing, and even the street lights and porch lights offered only shadows.

After he had stopped at a dozen houses, he began jogging, too fast at first and then slower, keeping to a pace he could sustain for some time. His jeans rubbed against his knees, but he forced himself into an acceptance of them. He yelled her name into the night. Dogs barked in response. He circled through the playground of her elementary school, hoping that maybe she had walked there.

The walls of the school, like the houses surrounding it, leaned up against the night, turning charcoal in the lakes of light cast from a hidden moon. That little bit of light had no power to show where the little girl had gone.

He shook off the arresting thoughts of a terrible violence, a paralysis in time latent with impotence, and held tight to a thought that something wanted him to find her.

He ran through alleys and down the middle of empty streets, calling her name. The town hushed around him, porch lights flashed, a figure peered from a bedroom window, more dogs answered his calls. He ran in increasing circles, clockwise around the neighborhood. Each circle he expanded by two blocks as though gridding a fire, making certain that every square foot was covered before searching a new area.

He thought of little other than Grace huddled in some corner of the night holding tight to her Gi-Gi. His mind worked without randomness, however, having involuntarily shifted into the automatic.

Someone walking her dog down the street crossed when she saw Barnes running in her direction. Barnes slowed and asked if she had seen a little girl alone with a dog. The woman uttered a "No," and quickly went on her way.

He continued to run. Up the street. Past closed houses. Plastic trash cans, parked cars, blind garage doors, wooden picket fences like columns of dead flowers. Rows of frame and brick houses descended into the night. The voices of others calling her name. But not her voice answering. The houses, small fortresses broken by alleys connecting block to block. Street sign sentinels like bare trees. Lit and unlit doorways, potted plants, ceramic and cement animals. An abandoned lawn mower halfway through its job.

Running. The shifting qualities of dark and light deceived him, and more than once he thought he saw Grace move within the shadows. Only to find a plastic bag grasped within the limbs of a bush or a stray dog checking trash cans. Scaring a scavenging raccoon once as it robbed from a compost pile.

Running. He felt her receding from him, disappearing in magnitude. He stretched his vision into the gloom of the night and saw shadows.

A police car passed him driving the other way. It slowed and turned and pulled in ahead of him. The driver stepped from the cruiser and held out his hand for Barnes to slow.

"You out looking for the little girl?" he asked.

"Yes," Barnes answered, hopeful and out of breath. "Yes. She found?"

"No. I had to be certain—you're not dressed for jogging."

Barnes rested his hands on his knees and lowered his head. He breathed deeply to catch his breath before continuing.

"Cases like this," the officer said, "the kid usually is found hiding someplace."

The police officer said "Good luck" as he drove away. Barnes lifted a hand and returned a noncommittal wave, then set his pace again.

Barnes ran, increasing the crescent of his circle. His legs worked against the pull of the denim jeans he wore, and his lungs ached. A sudden shift of wind swirled around him. He looked into the darkened yards.

When the thought entered his mind, its whisper echoed gently. He slowed, thinking his mind was playing games with him, that his body had tired of the chase and had sent a signal to his mind to find a way out. Then, after he conceded the possibility, he wondered if he could take the chance of turning back to the house, that maybe she was just a block away or around the corner up ahead.

He turned and started back, his legs renewed and working with the possibility of youth. Up ahead in the night and coming toward him, Barnes could see the bouncing spots of light from the flashlights of other searchers. They momentarily reminded him of a night shift on a fire with firefighters wearing head lamps to spot the ground they worked.

The centuried bells in the tower at St. Joseph's Catholic Church rang in Sunday morning. Their sound ring formed a paean to the new night. Barnes heard their sound, but registered only the strike of each ring and not the time they measured.

He ran past a pair of searchers without offering any explanation and could feel their gaze follow him back toward the house. Taking the stairs to the front porch in two strides, his feet nearly slid from beneath him as he reached the closed front door.

"Ruth?" he called as he entered.

A lack of breath left him unable to say anything else. Stopping for just a moment in the home's entry, he stood with hands on hips and knees slightly bent. He could feel that last inch of lung fight against his breathing.

No answer. A single table lamp was on in the front room, but nobody sat near it. A car passed on the road outside, the beam from its headlights rolling across the room.

He walked down the hallway and through the kitchen to the basement staircase. Another darkness greeted him when he opened the door, and he felt certain that he had been wrong, that his instinct to return was not right.

He flipped on the light and walked down the dozen steps. The half-basement was unfinished, wooden beams, exposed pipe, and a cold cement floor. Boxes piled three and four deep lined one wall, two file cabinets stood alone against another wall like discarded ideas. An ancient Ideal water heater nearly as large as a Volkswagen car and the assembly of pipes converting it from coal to gas. A couple of chairs with torn upholstery, a folding card table, the frame to an oak acorn bed, retired radios and clocks, a life-size plastic Santa.

Nothing but the sediment and shadows from the many lives of the house.

Barnes searched quickly through the assortment and accumulation of castoffs for something that would signal a door, another room, the stile into Grace's secret place. Nothing. Nothing that made a door. Nothing other than concrete walls.

Except down near the floor, almost hidden in the shadow of the water heater, was the cast door to the old coal room.

Barnes bent down to open the door. It pulled easier than he

thought it would. The flicker of a light threw a soft rectangle through the opening.

Barnes lay down and crawled into the ambry, having to angle his shoulders to fit through the opening. Lit only by an upturned flashlight, the room looked sheathed in a charcoal haze. Wandering shadows danced across the low ceiling. Even prone on the floor, Barnes could see that the room stood no taller than he and was narrow enough for him to touch opposite walls with his arms outstretched. This was Grace's secret place.

This was where she came to control the world outside. In her one small place of freedom from the paralyzing possibilities of life, she sat rocking back and forth in her small chair, searching through what must have been the inexplicable losses of her world.

She sat on a small chair, rocking her little body into and out of the circle of light from her flashlight. In her arms, she cradled a tiny pink doll within the folds of her blanket, her Gi-Gi. Harp lay next to her, his head on his paws and his eyes watching Barnes. His tail flopped lazily when he recognized Barnes.

"Grace?" Barnes asked because he had lost every other word.

She did not answer. Instead, she continued to rock, and she looked into the flashlight. Her eyes remained steady and intent on that single light as though to look away might bring a darkness.

Barnes pulled himself completely into her room and kneeled facing her with the light between them.

"Grace?" Barnes asked again.

She blinked and still did not swerve her eyes. She said, though, almost so low that Barnes would not hear, "Daddy's gone forever. Grandpa is dying."

Her voice wedged its way into the retreating silence.

She looked at Barnes then, and Barnes could see that she had been crying and that she was about to cry again.

"Your grandfather is out looking for you," Barnes said.

"But he's dying."

"Yes, he is. But he'll be with us for a long time before then, and he wants to spend as much of that time with you as he can."

"And Daddy. Will he come home?"

"I don't know, sweetheart. All I know is that your mother is worried and scared, and she wants you."

The softness of a silence interrupted them again.

And Barnes said, "We all love you, sweetheart, and your mother and Call—we all need you."

Not quite a smile but a recognition of a smile formed on her face, and with watery eyes she stood and walked the few steps to Barnes. Still on his knees, Barnes lifted Grace in his arms, lifted her above him toward the ceiling and their mutual smiles brought her safely back down into his arms.

Barnes closed his eyes, losing himself in Grace's laughter. When he opened his eyes again, he watched the slow-motion movements of Grace and Call dancing in the silence of the front room.

The police had left nearly an hour earlier, and the neighbors had been thanked and were back in their beds.

Ruth had been upstairs when Barnes entered the house, and by the time she came down the stairs, Barnes had already left for the basement. She had stood alone in the imminence of her destroyed hope until she heard Grace's voice and then saw Grace being carried on Barnes's hip.

She cried and knocked Barnes back a step when she embraced both him and Grace. The police were called, the search ended, and Call rushed into the house. Deep lines like the furrows across a ranch road crossed the umber skin of his forehead, but his smile broadened noticeably when he saw Grace.

Call paused in the half-light of the entryway to look down on Grace. He had stood there once without any words to say after the fire that had killed half of Barnes's crew and Barnes sat in the same chair telling them what had happened. And maybe he had stood in that very spot with Ruth sleeping in the curl of his arm or thirty years later with Grace doing the same. And he may have stood there with tears in his eyes as he looked down on Ruth and thought how hard it would be to tell your daughter that her mother had died. And he stood there, exhausted and with his hands limp at his sides and his mouth open as though beginning a short prayer, before he kneeled and took Grace in his arms.

Grace was hugged, and chastised, and hugged, and hugged again.

Not more than fifteen minutes past two o'clock by the bells at St. Joe's Church, Barnes rolled out his sleeping bag on the grass of his backyard. He had already laid out a survival blanket for protection against the moisture and cold of the ground, and he placed his bag on top of that. He stripped off his shirt and boots and lay on top of the bag with his head resting on his hands.

He saw Maria Lopez walk past him to join the semicircle of ghosts stretching out on the grass with him. He saw Maria Lopez from a different angle, saw her eyes open, and could remember how vivid they were in life, black as Apache tears.

And he saw Warner bent as in prayer, Doobie and Stress together as though dying were something communal, and Horndyke, and after Lopez alone was Freeze with the jumper Fleming, then Earl and Hassler, Budd, Sully, Dago, Max Downey, and finally Chandler.

And he saw Ruth sitting in the dark in Grace's bedroom, just sitting and watching her daughter sleep curled on her side with her hands together under her cheek and her golden hair spiderwebbed across her forehead.

His ghosts slept on the ground around him, as they had slept near him in fire camps when they were alive and ready for his wake-up call. He knew he would dream of them again. Maybe every night for a long time he would dream of them. And sometimes his dreams would still wake him. And that was no longer a bad thing.

He watched the light from the moon shine through the nearby elm trees to toss shadows on the side of his house. He looked up into the night sky. In the hazy edge of the Milky Way that stretched out like the hair of a mare's tail, he recognized an empyrean presence. He breathed lightly and rolled on his side to sleep.